N
GOLD-
COURAGEOUS
KINGDOM
EOAA
FAERIE FOREST
SHENHARAH
TORTHOTH
MOUNTAINS
BLACK
FOREST
TEARDROP
SEA
E
FALLEN
CITY
FAERIE FOREST
RETEIG
CRYING RIVER
HONORABLE
KINGDOM
S
Kathy M

MW00932094

Avonoa Series

The Secret of Avonoa
(Book One)

The Shadow of Avonoa
(Book Two)

The Heart of Avonoa
(Book Three)

The Traitor of Avonoa
(Book Four)

The Krusible of Avonoa
(Book Five)

Also:

People of the Storm
by HRB Collotzi

The Traitor of Avonoa

H.R.B. Collotzi

ISBN: 9781072830320
Library of Congress Control Number: 2019907385
Kindle Direct Publishing Platform

avonoa.com

This book is once again dedicated to my amazing husband and my wonderful children. Thank you for your sacrifices and unending support. Thank you for believing in me when I didn't believe in myself. Thank you for reading my books and tolerating my insanity. Thank you for your patience and love.

Contents

The Heart of Avonoa
Book Three in the Avonoa Series
Complete Synopsis with Spoilers

Tog and Hiro reluctantly return to Rakgar's lair from a recent assignment. Rakgar, meaner than Hiro has ever seen him, tells Hiro that the humans don't seem to fear dragons as much as they should. They are attacking dragons in increasing numbers. Rakgar orders Hiro to kidnap their Princess Anna in order to remind the humans how dangerous dragons can be. Hiro reluctantly agrees, but he argues that if she is harmed or killed for learning of dragon intelligence, King Philip will retaliate, with disastrous results. Rakgar decides to exempt the princess from punishment as a result of any dragons breaking their oath of silence.

Meanwhile, since Philip has told Anna that she must prove her loyalty to the kingdom by marrying the man of his choosing, he needs to decide whom she should marry. If anything should befall Philip, his sister's husband would be next in line for the throne. As plans proceed with the faeries to produce dragon poison in mass quantities, Philip and Torgon plot a fake coup in order to find out who they can trust enough to betroth to Anna.

Hiro shows up and tells Anna that he's been sent to kidnap her. He promises she won't be harmed. She goes with him willingly because she trusts him.

Torgon and Philip find a suitable husband for Anna, but they can't find Anna to make the introduction. Because Anna hasn't disappeared recently, as had been her way for a long time, Philip thinks something might be wrong now and sends out a search party. The search party finds evidence that Anna has indeed been abducted by a dragon.

Although they bicker and the kidnap was no joy, Hiro and Anna seem to enjoy each other's company. Along the way back to Rakgar's lair they find evidence that dragons are being attacked and killed while sleeping and that dragon ash is being collected. They find arrows tipped with a black substance.

When Hiro drops Anna back at Rakgar's lair, Rakgar's foul mood has lifted. He tells Hiro that Priya has returned after a long absence. Hiro tells Rakgar about the humans collecting dragon ash, most likely directed by Philip. Rakgar orders Hiro to investigate it with Priya.

While Hiro and Priya investigate, Priya asks Hiro why he feels so strongly about the human woman. Hiro can't explain himself. He wants to love Priya, but his heart remains soft against her.

The pair also finds evidence of the cause of dragon deaths in the form of arrows with a black substance on the tip. They take it to the centaur majishun, Rylan. When Rylan tells them it's made of flarote and dragon ash, they must confess the secret they know that eating too much flarote can kill a dragon. The centaurs Rylan and Ashel readily agree to keep the secret. Ashel tells Hiro that when the time comes, the centaurs will support him, but only him, in battle.

Hiro and Priya tell Rakgar about the poisoned killings at the hands of the humans, but he won't listen. He trusts the faeries as the dragons' allies. Hiro asks if he can take Anna back to her home and Rakgar agrees to let him.

Meanwhile, Philip delays his friend and royal general Torgon's plans to travel to the Great Northern Mountain by starting a search for his own bride. He meets a laundry maid he can't deny an attraction to, only to awkwardly learn that she's Torgon's sister. Torgon refuses his immediate approval and leaves Kingstor for the Great Northern Mountain to check on the dragon poison production. He tells Philip that he'll decide what to do about him and his sister when he returns.

On Hiro's way back to Kingstor with Anna, they come across fresh human tracks. They agree they should investigate the source of them. The tracks run northward, away from Kingstor. As they follow the humans' trail, Hiro's heart breaks for Anna. He wants to protect her from the potential danger ahead, so he insists they turn back and follow a different track.

Once his heart is broken, the fire in Hiro's belly begins to threaten to go out for no reason. He's able to keep it burning by releasing flame whenever it dwindles.

Hiro and Anna find a building where they assume humans are stockpiling poisoned arrows. They decide to destroy it, but Hiro needs help from the Ice Ruck, and he decides he must leave Anna to find her own way back to Kingstor Noble while he destroys the facility. While the Ice Ruck helps Hiro destroy the facility, the faerie Skorkot tries to kill Hiro with a poisoned arrow.

The Ice Ruck refuses to help Hiro track down human survivors and leaves him. Hiro finds Anna while tracking humans who escaped the attack. They say their farewells again and Hiro leaves her where Torgon and the other humans will find her.

After barely missing the black dragon, Torgon rides back to Kingstor with Anna to tell Philip that the entire stock of poisoned arrows has been destroyed. They'll have to start over. To help Hiro, Anna lies to Philip and Torgon, saying that she was kidnapped by a red dragon.

In the end, Priya meets with the old seer dragon dame Visi, and is somehow in possession of Hiro's heart.

I

Trouble

Don't think about her. Don't think about her. Don't think about...Oh forget it.

Hiro heaved a sigh and shifted his weight from back to front. He was already much more fidgety than Nagimon. Nagimon had been part of The Watch for three decades and was still mocked for never sitting still. The Watch must be part of the rock. Still as the mountains. Hiro gave up and flopped belly-down on the rock he had perched on. He heaved another sigh.

That tree reminded him of her. The one below him on the surface, under the floating mountains he watched over. Several vines with yellow leaves billowed from the leafy green tree. Just like her yellow hair did in the wind.

Ugh, disgusting, he thought to himself, but he knew he didn't think of her as disgusting anymore. *What would Tog think? What would Priya think? No,* he shook his head, hoping to dispel those thoughts. *I'd rather think of Anna than dwell on what anyone else thinks about her.*

Her. Anna. Princess Anna of The Noble Kingdom. A kingdom of humans who thought themselves above every other species. A human princess, and the dragon who fell in love with her. Her soft skin. The little bumps that rose from it when she got cold. The delicate little fingers she used to hold onto his claw as he flew with her. How could anyone think those miniscule little fingers would have the strength to hold onto anything?

Yet, those tiny digits had also gently cradled his heart after it broke and he gave it to her. He had to admit, when she threw it back at him, it had thumped against him with more force than he would have expected.

Ugh, stop thinking about her, he chided himself for the millionth time. *We'll never be together. I'll never be able to tell anyone my heart broke for her. No one will ever know. The claw has landed, or, 'it's done', as the humans say.*

The fire in his belly guttered. Again.

Not now! Hiro sat up straight. *No! No! NO!* He begged his insides to stop. The fire in his belly guttered dangerously low. If it went out, he would die. That's what happens to dragons. He had felt it happen as he lay imprisoned in a snowy courtyard of that human kingdom, before Anna saved him.

But what can I do? He searched around himself. *Perhaps if I hide a small flame?* He couldn't find a large enough boulder to hide the fire he might produce.

This struggle had happened often since his heart had broken for the human woman. He could never predict it. He couldn't stop it by sheer will. The only thing he could do to keep it burning was to express some fire. Producing fire might be seen by other dragons as an alert, but he had to do something to keep his going. This was a matter of burning, or freezing into ash.

Feeling justified, he covered his maw with his claws and burped a small flame. Unfortunately, it wasn't enough. The fire in his belly continued to shrivel. He belched more and more until a long, hot stream spewed directly from his throat. When he finally stopped the flame, he felt the fire within him burning as bright as ever. And he heard wings whooshing through the air.

Oh spit in Tarsa's eye, he grumbled to himself. *Here it comes.*

A large brown dan clattered onto the rocks next to Hiro. "Where?" he demanded, searching the rocks below them.

"Tram, I didn't—" Hiro began to answer, but he was cut off by more dragons landing behind Tram.

"Who sent the warning?" a bluish gray dan asked before landing behind Tram.

"It wasn't—" Hiro said.

"Tram, was it you?" another dark gray dragon asked. "Is it humans?"

"I don't know, Hiro sent the warning," Tram answered.

"No—" Hiro started again.

"Where?" the dark gray dragon asked again, but another grey dragon arrived.

"What's going on?" Hiro rolled his eyes, as his best friend Tog scuttled up the rocks next to the group.

"Hiro set off a warning," Tram said.

"I didn't—" Hiro started again.

"Yes, you did," the dark gray dragon argued.

"Where?" Tog asked. "Is it humans?"

"No, I—"

"Humans?" the bluish gray dan asked. "Are they attacking? What did you see, Hiro?"

"It was the attacking signal," Tram stated.

"No, but—" Hiro raised his voice, but no one listened.

"That's what I saw," the dark gray dan said. They kept their voices low and their eyes scanned the horizon, so none of them saw Hiro roll his eyes again.

"A small flame, increasing in size before a long, hot flame from the throat?" Tog asked.

"Yes," Tram answered.

"But—"

"Where are they?" Tog asked.

"IT WAS A MISTAKE!" Hiro yelled above the voices.

Everyone froze. One by one their heads snaked around to glare at Hiro.

"How could you possibly set off that specific alarm by mistake?" Tram asked, but the others saved Hiro the trouble of having to answer.

"There's no one attacking?" the bluish gray dragon asked.

"Doesn't look like it," the dark gray dragon's eyes bounced between Hiro and the quiet landscape beyond.

"False alarm?" Tog asked.

"Guess so," the bluish gray dragon answered, his eyes narrowing at Hiro. "What would make you do that?"

"Forget it!" Tram spoke firmly to end the discussion. "Hiro, the signal has been sent. You need to go now and stop everyone from gathering to fight. Get to the Inner Mountain and explain yourself to Rakgar. Everyone else, back to your posts." Bunching his legs under him, Tram sprang from the floating rock into the air. Hiro could hear him muttering under his breath about watching over a fledgling as he flew away.

The two gray dragons flew away with similar curses under their breath. Hiro turned to Tog.

"Don't worry about it," Tog said. "I'm sure it could happen to anyone." Hiro sighed and opened his mouth to reply, but Tog cut him off again. "But, you'd better get going. Rakgar's not going to be happy."

Hiro rolled his shoulder and jumped into the air. Feeling the warm summer air in his wings made him realize he was definitely not cut out to be part of The Watch.

"False alarm! False alarm!" Hiro repeated as he flew toward the Inner Mountain. As he shouted, he heard others echo the refrain, so the message spread quickly. He flew through the floating rock of the Rock Clouds to land near the bottom of the Inner Mountain where Rakgar's lair faced the east.

"False alarm!" he shouted over the tumult he encountered upon entering the leader's cave. Dragons scurried in and out. Some carried flarote in their claws, returning the little bulbous plants to where they grew in the cave. Others were talking, some pacing, some barking orders, but most were whipping their tails for a fight. A few stopped in the middle of drying meat with their fire. Those cast a glance at Rakgar to see if they should continue.

Rakgar, the only dragon perfectly calm, sat on the floor of the cavern watching the others. When Hiro raced in with the exclamation of "False alarm!" Rakgar sat up straight.

"What do you mean?" he bellowed over the noise. Everyone stilled.

"It was a false alarm," Hiro said, almost in a whisper.

Rakgar's eyes narrowed. He glanced at the dragons drying the meat. "Take that to the feeding grounds," he said. "Go back to your assignments," he announced to everyone else.

Having finished his task, Hiro turned to leave.

"Hiro," Rakgar growled.

Before turning, Hiro forced his pinched face to relax from the frustration he felt. "Yes, Rakgar?" he asked in what he hoped was an even tone, devoid of guilt.

"Who sent the warning signal?"

Hiro hesitated. He had never been any good at hiding his feelings from Rakgar. He'd never really tried. And Rakgar had always been understanding, until recently. Hiro allowed himself to be jostled by dragons clattering from the cave. Taking a few steps toward Rakgar, he took a deep breath.

"I did," he answered.

Rakgar's eyes narrowed again. Hiro became distinctly aware of how large the mighty, gray dragon truly was. He understood how so many other dragons were intimidated by the many layers of horns and spikes surrounding Rakgar's head and shoulders. Rakgar resembled a terrifying stone lion with wings. In that moment, he looked like a dangerously hungry lion and Hiro felt like a trapped mouse.

"What did you see, Hiro?"

Hiro's head dipped. He debated with himself about whether to pretend he had actually seen something. Perhaps that was the reason he had taken a position on The Watch. He wondered if Rakgar would take the human and faerie threat more seriously if he thought Hiro had seen something dangerous. Of course, Rakgar would request his memory and his ruse would fall apart. Hiro would have to find another way to get through to Rakgar. Instead he mumbled, "I saw nothing, Rakgar."

"It's not an easy signal to set off accidentally."

"I know."

"It was designed that way for a reason. For *this* reason." Rakgar waved his claw at the dragons still loping from the cave with whispered comments, none of them positive, directed at Hiro.

Hiro felt their eyes on his back as dragons drifted past him. "I know, it's just..." he hemmed. He couldn't tell Rakgar the truth. He couldn't tell anyone the truth. How could he ever explain?

"Just what, Hiro?"

"I'm not...uh...feeling well." *That's the truth*, he thought. It had been a life or death moment when he loosed the fire that started the false alarm. Not feeling well was an understatement.

"Not feeling well?" Rakgar asked through slits for eyes. Hiro hung his head to avoid looking at Rakgar. "In what way?"

"Uh, it felt like my fire was going out." *Is that too close to the truth?*

"Have you eaten?"

"A couple days ago."

"You should be fine, but perhaps you should eat again soon, just in case."

Hiro nodded and turned to leave.

"Hiro," Rakgar called again. "Do you still want to try being on The Watch?"

Hiro paused. Barely able to meet the leader's eye, he answered, "Perhaps, I'm not suited for it after all."

"What were you thinking?" Tog had come straight to Hiro's cave once his turn on The Watch had ended. Now he glared at his friend while questioning him.

"I wasn't thinking," Hiro muttered into his claws. "I think that's been established."

The two dragons lay curled on the floor of Hiro's cave. Hiro had taken recently to the habit of lying in a bed of plush grasses, similar to the feeling of the floor of Jarek's barn. But he shifted as the same uncomfortable feeling attacked his insides again. His fire wavered.

"I understand if you're not feeling well, Hiro." Tog watched over his best friend with concern as Hiro coughed up more flame. "Why didn't you tell me, or someone else?"

"I didn't want to bother you with it," he answered. "I thought I would be fine."

"What's wrong with you, anyway?"

"I'm not sure," Hiro said truthfully. "I keep getting the feeling that the fire in my belly is going to go out."

"I said I understand not feeling well, but to feel like you're dying? That's pretty serious." Tog's brow creased. "Perhaps you could ask Rakgar for more flarote."

Hiro shook his head. "I've had too much already." That was a lie. When Hiro had returned Anna to Kingstor and come back to the Rock Clouds in the spring, flarote was the first cure he tried for whatever had happened to him. However, upon eating one little bulb, his fire burned so hot and bright he thought he might burn to ash from the one dose. Yet in the next moment his fire guttered again. After that he either pointedly refused or hid any other offers of flarote.

Flarote was a wonderful little plant. It could heal almost every animal and save even dragons from certain death. However, for dragons it was a double-edged sword. A small amount of flarote eaten could heal them, but if they ate too much, it would kill them. With Hiro's fire threatening to go out, there was no point in risking death. He already knew it couldn't heal a broken heart.

"It's happening more often." Hiro rolled onto his side and scratched at his belly. "I don't know what to do anymore."

"How often does this happen?" Tog asked, watching his friend.

"Several times a day now," Hiro said.

"When did it start?"

That was the question Hiro had anticipated and dreaded most. "A few weeks ago," he answered, hoping to evade the truth. Unfortunately, Tog was smarter than he was vague.

"That's when you were with Anna."

Hiro rolled his shoulder in a shrug. "I guess."

"Do you think she did something to you? Poisoned you in some way?" Tog asked.

"Anna wouldn't do that," Hiro sighed.

"That you know of," Tog muttered, resting his head on his claws. "Wait," he lifted his head again, "what did you eat while you were with her? You were gone so long, you must have eaten something."

"I had some lydik with the centaurs and some lion while Anna and I were on the trail of those human men."

"The men you slaughtered?"

"No," Hiro said, "we never caught up to the ones we were following. We killed the smaller group at the encampment with Skorkot."

Hiro remembered it well. His heart had broken and he insisted that following the first set of men further north would be too dangerous for Anna. He remembered getting help from the Ice Ruck to destroy the little wooden buildings. After the Ice Ruck left, he had tracked down Anna and taken her closer to home before leaving her to find her own way back.

"I wonder if..." Hiro started, but let his voice trail off.

"What?" Tog perked up again. "What is it, Hiro? Anything might be a cause at this point, no matter how unimportant it might seem."

"Well, I wonder..." How could he possibly voice the concern to Tog without letting him know that his heart had broken for the human? "I was with Priya before I took Anna back to Kingstor."

"Yes?" Tog encouraged any talk of Priya these days.

"I have to wonder... if my heart broke for her," Hiro tried to sound curious. He was attempting innocence. Tog's heart broke before Hiro's had, for a dame named Surneen. Hiro knew Tog would naturally feel like the more experienced one in this situation. "I don't know what it feels like. Maybe it did and I didn't notice."

Tog laid his head back down. "It doesn't work like that, Hiro. When your heart breaks, you'll know. Without a doubt, you'll know."

"But maybe I didn't notice," Hiro pressed on, "or maybe it was in the process of breaking for her, but never finished..."

Tog flicked his tail. "I'm telling you, it doesn't work like that. It's instantaneous. One echoing, cracking sound inside your head and all of a sudden you're spitting out your heart. It's not like it could stop halfway between the crack. Besides," he grinned, "I've never felt better in my life. After my heart broke, I felt like I could go three sun cycles fighting Rakgar." Tog adopted a dreamy glaze in his eyes, obviously not thinking about fighting their leader.

"Speaking of hearts breaking," Tog stood and stretched his front legs, "I should probably be getting back to Surneen. She may be back from her hunt by now." He stopped thinking about his mate and looked Hiro in the eye. "Be sure to let me know if it gets any worse." When Hiro nodded, Tog drifted out the front of the cave.

Hiro groaned. This wasn't something that happened after a dan's heart breaks. Tog felt wonderful after his heart broke. He never once complained about dying. So, what was happening to Hiro?

2

Betrothal

Philip watched as Torgon leafed through more papers. "Here's another one," the royal general mumbled through a thick bite of cheese. "Province Uerting." He glared at the paper. "Says since they're so far east, they will march straight to the Rock Clouds..." he put the paper down with a sigh, "as requested. They've almost arrived at Shenharah."

Philip stood next to a large map hanging on the wall in the war room. Torgon sat at the table with papers and charts and smaller maps in front of him, as well as a large plate of meats and cheeses. As they were alone together, following the course of the provincial squads and their movements, Torgon sat back in the chair casually, resting his feet on the table, ticking off the numerous groups and their whereabouts.

"I wonder," Philip muttered as he pushed a pin into Shenharah. It sank a little further than he intended. "Do they know what they're going up against? Shouldn't I speak to the armies? Did they even notice...?" His voice tapered off.

"Notice that the summons didn't come from their king?" Torgon finished the thought while brushing crumbs from his lap. "I doubt it." When Philip turned a dubious eye on his best friend and royal general, Torgon continued. "The faeries have the means to send orders that look like they come from you anyway. At least you know what they're sending. Somewhat."

"The idea, if not the details." Philip turned slowly back to the map. Taking in the several blue pins and outlying reds and golds, he voiced his deepest fear to his closest ally. "When did I lose my kingdom, Torgon?"

Torgon stood from his chair, sweeping his black hair out of his eyes. "You haven't lost your kingdom, my friend. The provinces react only because the faeries invoke your name; they wouldn't be moved to act for any other reason. They are loyal to only you."

"But I am forced to operate according to the faeries' will," Philip's teeth ground together as he said it. "They are the ones in control. Not me. My father would never have bowed to their demands."

Torgon took a step closer. "Yes, he would have." Philip finally met Torgon's eye. Pointing to the maps in front of them, Torgon spoke with more passion than Philip had ever heard from him before. "You are doing what is best for this kingdom. You are taking care of your people. The faeries threatened you, yes. But it's better for dragons to die for it, rather than humans."

"I still feel like a war is not the only option." Philip and Torgon had discussed this at length. He knew what Torgon would say.

"It's the only option you have. For now. Until you are presented with another, stop second guessing yourself. You're a good king and everything will be fine." Torgon bent over the papers in front of him and began dividing them into piles. "Unfortunately, I can't say the same about dinner."

Philip groaned and rolled his eyes. He'd almost forgotten about the upcoming awkward introduction he needed to make tonight between Anna and the man he'd chosen for her. "A fine friend you are," he said, motioning toward the nearly empty plate on the table. "If you won't be there to protect me, will you at least allow Tierni to join us?"

Torgon froze. It was the first time they had spoken of her since he'd returned. Torgon had left to check on Murzod, the wayward captain, and he'd promised that when he returned he would tell Philip whether he would allow his best friend to be involved with his young sister. Torgon's leave had not only been shortened, but it had turned disastrous and dangerous. When he returned, the two friends had much more important things to discuss, like war, supplies, and dragon attacks.

Torgon spread his hands on the table and stared down at them. "I had almost hoped you'd forgotten about her and moved on." It had been several weeks, and Philip had long assumed that was Torgon's desire. When Philip didn't answer, Torgon sighed and looked up at him. As the head of his family after his father's death, Torgon took his duties very seriously. "Tierni will not be joining you either. At least," he held up his hands in mock-defense, "not tonight. You will have to deal with those two on your own for now. And I'm sorry."

Philip's heart began to race, but he tried to relax his face, and hopefully appear impassive. "About what?" he asked, willing his voice not to crack.

"That I haven't given you an answer about my sister yet." Torgon gathered his things, placing the light cloak embroidered with the royal general's swords around his shoulders. "I'll answer you soon, I promise, but I don't think either Tierni or I need be subjected to what you will have to endure tonight."

Philip breathed again and gave him a half grin. "Dieko isn't that bad, is he?"

Torgon stopped in front of Philip on the way out the door. "It's not him I'm afraid of."

"Anna," Philip greeted his sister as she swept into the room with her usual grace. "You look well." He briefly rose from his seat at the dining table when she entered but sat again when she joined him. She automatically sat to his right, being the closest person to take over the kingdom should anything befall him.

Even if the other nobles would never allow it. "I marvel at how quickly you've recovered."

It was true. After only a couple days of recovery from her ordeal, her face had resumed its natural glow. The sunken cheeks had filled in with color. The dark circles under her eyes had vanished. The skip in her step had returned and with it, the aura of living a life of privilege with not a care in the world. No one would have guessed that just weeks ago she had been kidnapped by a dragon, fought her way to freedom, and struggled for weeks through harsh temperatures and rough landscape, to be found alone by Torgon next to the road, seducing death.

"I'm much stronger than you think," she repeated. It was the only answer she'd ever given when asked about her recovery.

"Indeed," he muttered again.

Anna's forehead pinched together quizzically when she saw that Philip's plate was empty. In the act of placing her napkin, she stopped. "Are we waiting for Torgon?" she asked.

Philip shook his head. His napkin wasn't placed on purpose. He'd told Murthur to wait on the food until Dieko arrived, and he'd asked Dieko to come in after he and Anna were seated. Now he needed to delay her from knowing the purpose of this dinner. "Someone else is coming."

Anna's delicate eyebrows lifted. "Oh? Do I know them?"

Philip paused to sip his water, but Anna continued to watch him closely. "You might have been introduced in court." He knew that wasn't entirely true. He knew well that Dieko had been introduced to Anna in court. Dieko had almost always been present since she came to the kingdom months ago. There was no possible way they couldn't have met, but Philip needed Anna to remain off guard.

Anna wouldn't have it. She tilted her head. "Shall we have a game of it, or are you going to tell me who it is?"

Philip sighed, glaring at his water glass. He was getting hungry. Where was that cursed man?

"Fine," Anna stated. "A game, then. Is it a man or a woman?"

Finally the doors opened and the two royals jumped at the sound. Dieko stepped through them wearing a heavily gilded jacket and a dark cloak with gold stitching covering the shoulders and hems. The high shine on his tall boots reflected beaming rays of light. He'd even worn his sword. He obviously wanted to make an impression on his wife-to-be.

Philip stood. "Lord Dieko of Selevyn," he said for Anna's benefit. "So glad you could join us."

When Dieko saluted with his fist to his chest, Philip noticed the fist wasn't turned properly; the salute sloppy in stark contrast to his polished appearance. The nobleman bowed, saying, "I apologize for my tardiness, My King, and request to join you at your dinner table." He continued to stand at the foot of the table opposite Philip while Anna stared at him openly with astonishment.

"Of course, you are most welcome, sir," Philip answered formally, gesturing for the man to be seated as Anna spoke.

"Lord Dieko," she said, "I believe we have met in court. I recall you being in attendance several times these past months."

"Yes, My Lady," Dieko answered. "I've been in the Noble Kingdom since you arrived." He bowed to Anna but continued to stand.

"Dieko," Philip watched the man awkwardly shift his footing, "won't you be seated?" Philip spread his hands to indicate that he should sit, but Dieko remained at attention.

"I apologize, Sire, but..." the older man glanced at Anna, "I believe she's in my place."

Tradition dictated that the husband-to-be sit to the right of either the king or the king and his wife, where Anna sat now, but the betrothal had not yet been announced. Anna didn't even know—

"I'm sorry?" she said slowly in a low tone, but it was like a knife slicing the air. Her eyes bounced between Philip and Dieko.

Dieko, not even feigning innocence, turned beady eyes on Philip. "Haven't you told her yet?"

"Anna," Philip swallowed what felt like a pillow, "Dieko is the man I've chosen to be your husband."

At this, Dieko's boots clicked on the stone floor when he walked over to stand behind Anna's chair, his rightful place.

She didn't make eye contact with either man. "So, you've decided, then?" When Anna finally looked at

Philip, he nodded. She rose in such a swift motion Dieko didn't have time to pull out her chair. Instead, it bounced against his belly as she stood. He caught it and stabilized himself and the chair. "Then I *am* in his seat."

For a moment, Philip thought she was going to turn to escape out the doors at the end of the table, but she walked around to the other side in silence. Dieko waited beside the vacant chair. Philip stood and, once Anna waited for a servant to pull out the chair across the table for her, the three seated themselves slowly.

"We don't usually stand on tradition at this table," Anna said as she sat, "but if we were to do so now, shouldn't you remove your weapon?"

"Not so," Dieko answered, placing his napkin. Although Philip was taller than most—standing well above most of the men in the kingdom—Dieko seemed to be straining his back and neck to match his height. "I wouldn't expect you to know Noble protocol, nor a Nobleman's protocol. As I understand, you have lived in the mountains," he didn't look at Anna long enough to see her jaw grind, "so I shall explain. Every man should keep themselves armed in times of war. Even the king."

They both looked at Philip, Anna with incredulity, Dieko with poorly feigned caution. *Did he really just correct my behavior?* Philip thought to himself.

"We're not really at war, Dieko." He waved for the food to be served. "It's really more of an extended hunting holiday. If we were fighting other humans or centaurs, I would ..."

Before Philip could finish, Dieko recited, "Nobility Charter, chapter seventeen, article five, paragraph two,

'All males of acceptable martial age and expertise should be armed with either their weapon of choice or a sword unceasingly if the kingdom is at war or under imminent threat of danger. The king and his protectors, being the guards of the castle, should always wear swords on their hips if the kingdom is at war or under imminent threat of danger.'"

Silence. *He is correcting me. This had better not begin a habit,* Philip mentally noted.

Murthur began ladling soup. Every chink of the spoon to bowl or pot echoed in the dining room. Once the bowls were filled and served, Philip reluctantly lifted his spoon.

"I think," Anna said, breaking the silence, "the key word there is 'should'."

"Not necessarily," Philip said, satisfied to see her snap her head in his direction. "Yes, 'should' implies that it might not be possible to always have your sword upon your person. Nor that it is a binding rule to be followed with punishment if impugned. But I think another word offers more options of translation. Dieko obviously feels there is an 'imminent threat' to the kingdom. I, however, do not."

Anna relaxed her shoulders. With a barely perceptible smile, she picked up her spoon and tipped it into her bowl of soup.

Dieko, however, didn't touch his spoon. "You don't feel that another dragon could attack the kingdom at any moment, Sire? After so much has happened?"

"No, I don't." Philip sipped his soup.

"Well," Dieko finally leaned over his broth, "I understand how a female may not detect the approach of danger," Philip stole a glance at Anna and saw her lip twitch, "but I would expect a man, even one as young as yourself, to recognize a threat when you see one. There have been more dragon sightings in the past few months than the Noble Kingdom has seen in the past few decades put together. How can you not take that seriously?"

"You mistake me, Dieko," Philip said, resting his spoon next to his bowl. "I do take it seriously, but I choose not to live in fear that I will be attacked at any moment. If a dragon were immediately without these walls, you can be sure I would don my sword and keep a quiver on my back. In point of fact, I did live as such daily when we held the black dragon in the courtyard. But when there hasn't been a dragon sighting in weeks and, in fact, the last sighting was benign, I don't feel any reason to live with fear either in my heart or on my head. You, however, may live as you see fit."

Philip returned to his soup and was satisfied with a grunt of disagreement from Dieko and a full grin from his sister.

"Are you second guessing Dieko, or Anna?" Torgon asked as he walked alongside Philip down the corridor.

"Neither...both...I'm not sure." Philip knew he hadn't made much sense since dinner. He had gone to Torgon's suites to discuss what happened. They decided previously not to follow their nightly routine of chess in the hall so Philip could give Torgon a complete breakdown of the evening without Dieko within earshot. But from the moment he sat down in Torgon's anteroom, his thoughts and words had taken a turn for the worse. With Philip unable to sit still, the two friends decided that a walk through the quieter halls of the castle would help.

"Ok," Torgon took on the patience of a tutor with a difficult student, "what we know. Dieko wasn't overly kind to Anna?"

"Correct."

"And she took it in stride without lashing out."

"Also correct."

"Dieko took it upon himself to point out something he felt you should be doing." Philip narrowed his eyes at Torgon, who held up his hands in defense. "Erroneously."

"Correct."

Torgon took a deep breath in thought as they walked along, and clasped his hands behind his back. Their pace wasn't brisk, but it seemed to pick up every time Dieko's name was spoken. Torgon nodded. "It sounds as if Dieko is the one you're questioning, not Anna. Anna did nothing wrong."

"I'm questioning myself," Philip said. "Perhaps I'm going about this the wrong way. Perhaps I should let Anna choose a husband for herself."

"Who do you think she would choose?" Torgon asked, side-stepping a guard with a nod.

"I have no idea." Philip raked his fingers through his hair. "I don't think she knows whom to choose any more than I do. Dieko is the best option I can see. I may not like how he handles himself at dinner, but he's not treasonous, and that's the most important quality."

"Have you thought," Torgon slowed a little, "that perhaps Dieko is trying to take on the fatherly role with you?" Torgon shrugged as Philip's eyebrows shot up to his hairline. "Maybe he feels that's what you need since that piece of your life is vacant now. Or even that it might be what you're looking for in him." He allowed his shoulders to drop. "Maybe he's just trying to do what he thinks you want him to do."

Philip stopped in the middle of the hall. "I hadn't thought of any of that." He tried not to scuff his toes on the floor as he considered their conversation. "Maybe I should have a talk with Dieko."

Torgon nodded. "I don't think it would hurt the situation; however, I think there is someone else you need to speak with first." He held out one hand, pointing at where they had arrived.

Without realizing where their walk had taken him, the doors to Anna's suites stood before them at the end of the hall. Philip nodded. Without another word, Torgon spun on his heel and left.

Philip took a few steps forward. He didn't know what he wanted to say to her. He enumerated a few points in his head. He wanted to know if she was ok with the match. He wanted to know what she thought of

Dieko, even if her opinion might not change Philip's plans for their engagement. But then again, it might.

He stopped at her doors and knocked lightly. The hall was deserted.

Shouldn't there be guards outside her door? he thought briefly, but he was too pleased not to have witnesses watching him steel himself here that he didn't give it a second thought. He gently pushed the door open.

"Anna," he whispered into the sitting room. He had been inside her chambers only a handful of times in his life, but he knew where the other doors led. One led directly down a hall into Anna's dressing room. He knew he didn't want to go in there. The far door led to her sleeping chambers. No need to use that one either. The middle one, in the back next to a tapestry of faeries in celebration, led to a more informal sitting room attached to the sleeping area.

As he got closer, Philip realized the door was open, but was only barely ajar. Not wanting to walk in on her, he peeked through the doorway in time to see Anna and her maid, Amythyst, enter the sitting room from her dressing chamber.

"...change in a moment," Anna was saying to the maid. "This can't wait. I must speak to him."

Anna had clearly just arrived back in her rooms from dinner. She still wore her dinner gown of deep purple.

Is she talking about me? Philip thought. *Does she want to talk to me?*

Philip put his hand on the handle of the door, preparing to push it open, but stopped when he saw Anna sit down in front of a table against the opposite wall. A large mirror leaned against the wall. Philip shied away from the crack in the door for a moment, afraid Anna might see his reflection in the mirror, but Anna didn't look up.

"But my lady," Amythyst whispered, "will he come?"

Anna leaned down from the stool she sat on and pulled something from under the curtained table in front of her. When she sat up straight, Philip could see that it was a black velvet bag. She opened the drawstring at the top and pulled out a large black gem, the likes of which Philip had never seen before. Tapered at the top and bulbous at the bottom, it looked like a teardrop cut from a stone as large as a pineapple.

"He'll have no choice," Anna told the maid.

Philip's eyes widened as he watched Anna. She put the velvet bag on the table and cupped the gem in both hands. Gently, almost caressing it, she brought it next to her face. She whispered into the glistening facets that reflected the light of the candle on the table.

"Hiro, come to me," her voice pleaded into the gem. With a look of sorrow and longing, she replaced the gem in the velvet bag and secreted it away.

Philip turned his back to the door with his brows drawn in tightly to his eyes. Anger boiled inside him. *So many secrets,* he thought as he seethed. *She still keeps so many secrets from me. She'll obviously never offer them. Maybe Dieko will be able to get them out of her.*

3

Intimate Confidante

ANNA! Her name screamed inside Hiro's head. *GET TO ANNA!*

Yes, of course! I must! Without realizing, Hiro had jumped off the bed of grasses in his cave and tumbled to his cave opening. He spread his wings before he heard the voice.

"Hiro? What are you doing? Where are you going? Are you feeling better?" Prak ran up to Hiro. The black dragon wondered why the little brown dragon might be outside his cave at such a late hour of the day.

"Yes," Hiro answered without thinking. "I need to leave. I'm going to—" He was barely able to cut off his own voice. He'd almost told Prak that he needed to go see Anna.

Why would I do that? he thought.

"Rakgar wants to see you first," Prak cut into his thoughts, "wherever you're going. Come with me to the Inner Mountain."

Hiro's head spun. He had been resting in the cave. He had been dreaming of Anna. He heard her voice. He had to go to her. He couldn't go see Rakgar. He had to go to Anna.

"But—" Hiro started, looking beyond Prak to the dark, distant mountains.

"Just for a moment," Prak insisted. "Rakgar wants to see you. He's concerned about you, Hiro. We all are."

In the back of his mind, Hiro knew he should be concerned about that statement, but he wasn't. He had to get to Anna. Why were they delaying him? His eyes bounced between Prak and the mountains in the distance. He knew Anna was beyond those mountains. Could he even really see the mountains? But that's where he needed to go. He couldn't think of anything but leaving. Now.

"Fine," he said. He closed his eyes, trying to focus his thoughts on the present. "Just for a moment."

"Ok," Prak said, lifting into the air. "Follow me."

Follow him? Hiro thought again. *Why would I follow him? He's going the wrong direction. Anna is the other way.*

But he lifted into the air with Prak waiting for him ahead. Then suddenly his claws were touching the ground. They were walking into Rakgar's lair. Prak kept a watchful eye on Hiro from ahead, leading the way further into Rakgar's lair.

What am I doing here? Hiro's mind reeled as he watched Prak step up to Rakgar and whisper something. He knew again in the back of his mind that he should be concerned about it, but he wasn't. *This isn't where I wanted to go. How did I get here? Where's Anna? I need to go to her.*

"Hiro," Rakgar, now finished whispering with Prak, turned to face him. "Are you feeling alright?"

Hiro only shook his head. He couldn't trust his voice.

"Perhaps you should lie down," his leader said.

Hiro thought Prak had the strangest look on his face. *What is he so concerned about?*

"No, I need to leave," Hiro said. He scanned the surroundings without actually seeing them. Why were they delaying him this way? Couldn't they see he needed to leave?

"Where do you need to go, Hiro?"

Why was Rakgar talking to him with this concern? He couldn't tell Rakgar about Anna. Or did Rakgar already know? Who else knew about Anna?

"I just need to go, Rakgar," Hiro spat out. His tail twitched from side to side. He danced from one foot to the other. "South," he finally said.

"South?" Rakgar asked.

"Toward warmer weather?" Prak asked.

Rakgar nodded. "Perhaps warmer weather would do you some good. Our summer is unseasonably late in coming this year."

Prak nodded. "I could go with him and make sure—"

"No!" Hiro hadn't meant to shout. He lowered his voice. "I just need to get away. I need to be alone." No one else could come with him to see Anna. Not Prak. Not even Tog. No one would understand.

"Hiro," Rakgar said calmly, "you haven't been acting like yourself lately. I think it would be best if you had some company. You might not be safe on your own right now."

Prak took a step forward. "I don't mind going," he said. "We can go down south. Get some sun. See if we can find Priya. It'll be fun!"

Hiro took a deep breath and seized control. He had to get out of here. Alone. "Thank you, Prak. I appreciate it, but really, I just need to be alone. I'll be alright. I promise." He looked up at Rakgar and forced himself to hold a steady gaze at the leader. "Please, I want to be alone."

Hiro's mind spun like a fledgling on the wind while he waited. Rakgar stood perfectly still, staring down his snout at him. He glanced at Prak, who tilted his head. But when he looked back at Hiro he nodded. "Alright, Hiro. You're a fully accepted adult of this ruck. You have the choice to be by yourself if you wish. Go south. Kill something. You'll feel better."

Hiro barely composed and showed his gratitude before he tore out of Rakgar's cave. His wingtips brushed the edges of the cave opening as he launched himself into the dark sky without a second glance backward.

Why am I going so slowly? Rakgar said the summer was late coming this year. Is the cooler air slowing me? How long should it take me to get to Centaur River?

In the back of his mind, Hiro thought the sun should have come up by the time he reached Centaur River, but it was still as dark as pitch.

Have I been flying for an entire night and day? Why is this taking so long?

His mind churned. His head started to ache from thinking. Every time he thought of anything other than Anna, his head ached. But if he just flew, with nothing but thoughts of being with Anna, the pain would subside.

I must go to her. I must go to her.

Every wingfall beat out the statement. His wing joints began to ache from effort. He only pumped them harder.

The sky began to lighten. Gray seeped over the horizon.

No, he thought, *I must be almost there by now.*

He slipped through the Torthoth Mountains without a second thought of what he might see or encounter. He flew over the Hamees village where Jarek and Boorda lived. He flew over the smaller mountains that stretched from the Torthoth range to Teardrop Sea. The very mountains Anna had been born and raised in. He raced along the range until he met the waterfall on the border of the King's Forest. Without really thinking or planning anything, Hiro lifted further into the mountains, flying straight up the rocky crags. He set down at the top of a cliff overlooking Kingstor Noble and the castle with five towers.

One of the towers was part of Anna's chambers. Her window was high up and far away, but he could see it from this distance with the sun bright overhead. Was it finally daytime? Focusing on the small window, Hiro saw the signal. A bright red banner hung from the window. She was there. She was waiting.

Hiro looked at the sun shining over him. It was almost to its zenith in the sky. He scanned the forest below him and searched the towers and walls around it. No one had raised the alarm. No one had seen him. Even if they had, they hadn't stopped him. They hadn't shot at him. Everything was quiet. He had to risk going into the forest.

Sliding down the steep mountain rock face, Hiro slithered into the forest at the base of the mountain. It would take time, but he crawled through the trees, silent as a shadow. He paused occasionally to make sure no one had noticed him or stumbled into him. Several smaller game animals scurried close by in the forest, but nothing large or dangerous...except him.

Finally, after what felt like an eternity at his stealth pace, Hiro passed through a thick clump of trees to look down into a depression. A peaceful meadow lay before him, bathed in sunlight and covered in soft green grass. Boulders gathered together to one side and a small pond fed from a tiny trickle of water falling from the slopes beyond. A horse was tied up at the far side of the clearing. Next to the water sat Princess Anna.

Anna. Her golden hair was pulled away from her heart-shaped face. The delicate fingers of one of her hands dipped in the water of the pond. She sat casually in a gown of brilliant red with bright gold stitching on the hem, resting her other arm around her knees.

He should have waited to listen for danger. He should have circled the entire clearing and meadow to make sure they were alone. He should have sniffed the ground for signs of other humans having been there recently. He should have done all these things and more out of caution, but instead he burst from the trees and ran to her side.

"Hiro!" She looked up as he ran toward her. She brushed grass from her skirts and tried to look the dragon in the eye. "I didn't expect you so soon!"

As soon as he stood in front of her, the realization of what had brought him here with such urgency, what had happened, hit him like a boulder to his head. His mind cleared. His confusion disappeared. The overpowering force drawing him to her made complete sense.

"You used my heart to ..." he paused, "you called me, didn't you?"

"I had to," she said. "We need to talk."

"Do you know what I could have done?" he growled.

"I needed to see you," she protested. Then her eyes squinted at him. "What did you do?"

"I almost told everyone about you," he curled up on the ground. "I almost told Rakgar."

Anna blanched. "You didn't."

"No." Hiro took a deep breath, remembering the effort it took not to yell, "I have to go to Anna!" directly at Rakgar. "I didn't tell him or anyone else, but," he stared into her face, "I could have. I almost blurted it out just so I could get away on my own."

"On your own?" She gathered her skirts and stepped inside the curve of his front legs. Seating herself in his claws, she asked, "Why wouldn't they let you leave on your own? I thought you said that once you're an accepted adult in the ruck, you could do what you like."

"Not now," he said, shaking his head. "Once I told Rakgar about destroying the poison storage facility with the Ice Ruck, he banned anyone, other than approved hunting parties, to leave the Rock Clouds unless absolutely necessary. When I wanted to leave, he wanted to send Prak or Tog or someone with me."

"Why would he have to send someone with you? Doesn't he trust you?"

"Not like he used to," Hiro said. He couldn't tell Anna about the fits of his fire dying either. He hadn't worried her with that yet and there was nothing she could do about it anyway. She knew nothing about dragon anatomy. "But enough about that. What did you need to talk to me about?"

"My brother," she said with a huff.

"Have you figured out if he's the one making the dragon poison?" he asked. They had been over this before. Hiro and Priya had discovered that someone was making dragon poison. They didn't know who or how or where. Hiro and Anna had come upon a facility in the north that had barrels full of arrows dipped in the poison. That was the one they got the Ice Ruck to help destroy.

They knew the faeries were involved, especially since Rakgar's traitorous faerie advisor, Skorkot, had tried to kill Hiro at the facility in the north. Rakgar didn't have any more faerie advisors hanging around, but that didn't change the fact that faeries were meeting with humans and planning attacks on dragons with them. Namely, with King Philip of the Noble Kingdom—Anna's brother.

"No," Anna said, fixedly staring at her fingers wringing each other. "But I have discovered a way to find out."

Hiro narrowed his eyes. "A way to find out? Is it dangerous?"

Without looking up, Anna shrugged. "Not dangerous, but certainly...unappealing."

"Then don't do it." Hiro said it so sharply that Anna abruptly lifted her face up to meet his. "You've done too much already. This," he gingerly opened his claws from their position around her frame, "this is too risky. What would your brother, the king, do if he saw this?"

"Honestly?" she asked, standing up. She began to put her hands on her hips, a sure sign she was preparing to tell Hiro just exactly where his place would be, but they dropped to her side. "I have no idea." She shook her golden waves of hair around her and paced a small circle as she spoke. "I don't know what he would do. I would like to think that if he knew you could speak, that he would talk to you calmly and you would come to a mutual understanding of peace. But..." she sighed, "he's too deep in the faeries' cowls to know where his mind walks." Turning her bright green eyes on Hiro, she almost whispered. "He's decided I must marry."

"Marry?" Hiro's mind went numb. He felt as if he was hearing himself speak from far away. "Marry? Isn't that when two people tie a ribbon around their hands?"

One of her hands curled into a tiny fist. "Yes."

"That means..."

"Yes," she whispered again, "it is similar to you being mated."

"But then—" His voice sounded hollow. Empty. "Don't you have to choose your mate?"

"Royal women don't choose their mates." Anna's voice dropped so low Hiro had to strain to hear her over the sound of a grasshopper.

Hiro shook his head. He couldn't think. This couldn't be happening. "He would presume to choose for you?"

"That's how it's done." She sat in the crook of his claw, leaning her back against the bottom pad of it. "If he were a little older, or married, or..."

Hiro met her eyes. "Or what?"

"Or didn't feel like his life might be in danger," she finished, "then he might allow me to find someone on my own. But since the faeries and the...threats...I guess he feels like it needs to happen sooner rather than later."

"Sooner?" Hiro said. She nodded, but Hiro gurgled out a chuckle. "Sooner?"

"Yes?" She asked with a quizzical crease in her brow.

"But Anna," Hiro breathed a sigh of relief as the idea struck him, "*sooner* doesn't mean *now*, does it?"

Anna's brow crinkled more. "Well, no, but—"

Hiro growled a low laugh. "He still has to find an appropriate man, make sure you approve of him, plan the ceremony, and so forth." He laughed again. "You humans move so slow in everything you do, I'm guessing it will be more than five seasons before he decides on a suitable man for you."

Anna was silent a moment, then whispered, "His name is Lord Dieko of Selevyn."

Hiro froze. The fire in his belly guttered as if it had been stomped on. "Dieko?"

"Yes."

Twisting his head aside, he spit fire into the little pond. "Sounds like he would taste disgusting," he turned back to the princess, "but I might be willing."

"Willing to what?"

Hiro bared his fangs. "Willing to slowly chew his limbs off one by one."

Anna sighed. "I would love that," she said, staring into the sun descending into the trees around them. "But unfortunately, marriage to Dieko is the only way to learn anything about my brother's plans."

Hiro's fire rumbled to life again. "You don't have to do this!"

"I have to do something, and Philip tells me nothing that would help me, that would help you." She glared him in the eye. "I can't just sit in my castle and watch as the dragons are attacked when I know I could do something about it. At the very least, warn you what might be coming."

He glared back at her. He knew that look. That look in her eye meant she was about to tell him exactly what was going to happen. That look meant she would take control of the situation whether the big, dangerous dragon wanted her to or not. He ground his teeth, then relaxing his jaw, he said, "Then don't just sit there. Come with me."

Anna's eyes popped open. "With you? Where?"

Hiro's tail flicked as he thought. "The desert? The forest? The abandoned islands in the south? I don't care. Anywhere! Everywhere! Just you and me." He grinned in what he hoped wasn't a horrifying gesture. "I'll keep you warm."

She reached her hand out as if to stroke his face but shook her head and allowed it to swing back to her side. "No, Hiro. I'll have to make do with lots of blankets, lots and lots of blankets."

4

Significant Proclamation

Philip closed his eyes and took a deep breath. When he opened his eyes, he saw only the red circle out 30 paces in front of him. He lifted the tip of the arrow to point at the outer white circle. With another breath, he straightened his fingers and the arrow flew.

"Dead center," Torgon said as Philip lowered his bow. "I'll never understand how you do that, every time."

Philip scanned the target several yards away, but it was Ruther who answered. "And he probably can't explain it to you," Ruther said with a grin. "It's something that comes naturally." Ruther called the clear and ran out to collect the young king's practice arrows.

"That's not to say that it can't be taught," Torgon said.

"Of course not," Philip agreed while unstringing his bow for the day. "But it would take a better teacher than myself. And I'll never be as good at sword-play as you, but that's not to say I won't try."

"I, however," Torgon took the unstrung bow and passed it to Ruther when he returned, "will never try to be as good as you at the bow. I prefer fighting up close. I'll allow you to cover my back."

Philip paused in the act of removing his bracers in order to clap Torgon on the shoulder. "And I always will, my friend."

Torgon nodded. "I know. That's why I'm going to allow you to see Tierni."

The bracers dropped from Philip's hands. Hoping to cover the fumble, he swept up a towel to dab his face. The increasing warmth outdoors at the target range had nothing to do with the heat rising in his cheeks now. Philip's mind raced. He could see Tierni again. He could stare into those beautiful blue eyes all day long if she would let him.

But how to ask her? he thought.

Realizing he was standing completely still and holding a towel over his own face, Philip pulled the towel away to look at Torgon.

"Oh, uh—" he stumbled for words as he slowly wiped his neck and head.

"Don't tell me you're no longer interested, because—"

"No! I am!" Philip dropped the towel. "I mean, I do. I— I would like to— I mean—"

Torgon laughed. "I can honestly say I've never seen you this way about anyone or anything. I've seen you flustered and frustrated, but never this much. And certainly, never over a girl. You must be smitten."

Philip chuckled too. "I must. I mean I barely know her, but I would love the chance to find out."

"Woah, woah, woah," Torgon threw his hands up. "Let's get one thing out of the way right now. I am your friend—your best friend—and you can talk to me about anything...except Tierni."

"Right. Right. Understood." Philip nodded and searched around them. He saw that his belongings had been cleared but he hadn't noticed Ruther doing it, so he stood swaying uncertainly on the spot. Not sure what to do next, Philip turned toward the castle. After taking a few steps, he glanced up at Torgon.

"Thank you," he mumbled.

Torgon met his thanks with a large, toothy smile. "You're welcome. I just hope you don't embarrass yourself like that in front of her."

As Ruther pinned a heavy blue cloak around his shoulders, Philip's mind raced. He didn't think about the formal royal ensemble he was being fitted with. Instead, he mused to his servant, "How do I ask her?" as the man applied a brush to the cloak.

"Do you wish her to dine with you tonight?" Ruther asked as he brushed.

"No!" Philip hadn't meant to snap, but his tone stopped Ruther mid-stroke. "No," he said again, a little gentler as the brush moved again, "I don't think Dieko would appreciate dining with a servant." Ruther lowered the brush slowly and turned away from Philip. "I mean, Dieko isn't— he just doesn't—I don't think Tierni would—"

"Sire," Ruther's voice remained calm and steady as he turned to look Philip in the eye, "who are you ashamed of? Dieko? Or Tierni?"

Philip took a step back. "I'm not ashamed of either of them." His brow creased. "At least, not entirely." Ruther's gaze didn't waver, but Philip's slid to the ground as he did an internal search. *Why don't I feel comfortable with both Dieko and Tierni having dinner with me at the same time?* he questioned himself.

He finally brought his eyes back to Ruther's. "Would you or Murthur be uncomfortable serving Tierni dinner?"

Ruther sighed. "As your servant, this is my home. I happily serve those I care for in my home. And I care for the people you care for. That is my job and my life. As long as you care for Tierni, I will always serve her happily."

Philip nodded, with a grin tickling his lips. Then a thought occurred to him. "And Dieko? Will you serve Dieko happily?"

Ruther's smooth demeanor slipped for a moment. He tilted his chin and answered quietly. "If I'm not being too bold, Sire, occasionally I tolerate strangers in my home as well. But I always keep an extra close eye on them."

A chill ran down Philip's spine. This was why he liked Ruther so much. The man was more willing than his brother to speak his mind to the king. Philip enjoyed the frank conversations with those surrounding him. Honesty was always better than acquiescing agreement.

He nodded as his eyes wandered to the mirror. With a shock he inspected his clothing more closely. "And this?" he asked, flicking a hand at his reflection. "Will you tolerate this?"

Ruther's steady gaze creased with concern. "It is the appropriate dress for a formal royal announcement." He fussed over nonexistent lint and wrinkles.

"I'll faint from heat in this heavy cloak!" Philip insisted. "Can't I wear the lighter one? Or no cloak at all?"

"Sire!" Ruther's shock was apparent in his large eyes. "You must wear your station when making such an announcement. You know this."

"No, I don't," Philip admitted. "I've never made such an announcement before." Searching his reflection, he finally turned away with a grunt. "And thank the gods that I never will again."

"...A glorious day for the Noble Kingdom and for myself..." Philip read from the parchment in front of him without thought for the words he delivered. Instead, he focused on the sweat trickling down his spine and inwardly decided he would be more insistent on wearing less burdensome clothing the next time he made a royal announcement.

Torgon stood on the other side of Anna to Philip's right. Torgon wore only a light half-cloak on one shoulder. Although Philip noted that they both wore the same sword on each hip and a ceremonial knife in a blue sheath across their chests, Torgon's clothing was much lighter in texture and layer.

"...announcing the marriage of my newly discovered sister, the Princess Anna..." Philip lifted Anna's left hand in his right and guided her across to stand at his left side, in front of Dieko. The expression on her face hadn't changed since he'd first seen her that day. The color in it was as pale as the soft blue dress she wore. Her golden hair tumbled down over her bare shoulders. The silver circlet on her forehead sparkled like crystal in the summer sun. She didn't seem to be sweating.

Do women ever sweat? Philip asked himself. *Or does she look so cool because she gets to wear silk whenever she pleases?*

"...to Lord Dieko of Selevyn. The House of Selevyn has long been..." Dieko, also standing to Philip's left, wore a black fur half-cloak with gold tassels. Tassels! Philip didn't think Dieko was required to wear long boots and heavy breeches, but he did.

Philip started to lift Dieko's elbow as custom dictated, but it rose with so much leverage by straightening his back that Philip had to wave his hand under the older man's elbow to guide him across to his proper place on his right.

Back straight, hands folded on one hip, Dieko didn't smile. He didn't look at Philip or Anna. He touched no one. He looked at no one and his eyes hovered above the crowd gathered below.

"...in one month, these two shall be made one in the sight of the gods and under my own direction. The House of Selevyn shall become the Royal House of the Noble Kingdom." Despite the heat and choice of wardrobe, Philip's body threatened to shake as a cold chill ran through him.

With the announcement of the engagement complete, Philip turned back from the balcony overlooking the town in front of the castle. He had made royal announcements from that balcony before, but never one of marriage. He usually stayed and waved at the crowd until Murthur or Ruther motioned with a couple fingers to signify that he could leave. In this case, he was relieved to leave the newly engaged couple to face the crowd without him.

As soon as he gained the interior of the castle, he ripped off the heavy cloak and glared at Torgon waiting inside then turned the fierce look on Ruther. Tossing the cloak at the servant, he muttered, "You're never allowed to dress me for ceremony again."

Ruther's face fell as he draped the cloak over his arm. "And who else will? Especially if Murthur has other business!"

"You can take care of any other business for Murthur, until you can learn to dress me according to the season, no matter the occasion." Philip pulled off the heavy blue vest over his shirt to reveal sweat marks dripping down his front and back.

Torgon laughed as Anna finally stepped in from the balcony. Noticing Philip in only his undershirt, she pursed her lips at him. "Really, Philip. Must you disrobe in public?"

"This is the *inside* of my home, not open to the public," Philip complained. "And I'll strip down to nothing if I'm forced to dress this way again." He directed the last bit at Ruther.

"Will you at least dress for dinner later?" Anna asked, exasperated.

"Of course," Philip held his head up, "but I'll choose what I wear. Will you be joining us, Dieko?" Philip asked the nobleman as he stepped inside beside Anna. Philip noticed Anna tense slightly when she felt the man's presence.

Dieko grimaced openly at the state of Philip's undress and Ruther holding the discarded clothing. Lifting his nose in the air, he said, "Not tonight, Your Majesty. I need to see to arrangements in the city. I need to prepare for Anna's arrival in my home, among other business. I'll be away for a few days."

With a nod, Philip said, "You'll always be welcome at my table, Dieko. Return when you can."

As Dieko turned to leave, something clicked inside Philip. He wasn't listening as Anna reminded Dieko to say his farewells to her as well. Instead his mind swam with the possibilities of Dieko's absence at dinner.

"Ruther," he said in a low voice. "I wonder if it might be possible for you to...I mean to say, could you perhaps...some kind of invitation...it wouldn't have to be formal...I just don't—"

"You mean for Mistress Tierni?" Ruther deduced and Torgon grinned.

Philip could only nod.

"I'll speak to her myself, Sire," Ruther answered. Gathering up the clothing he held in his arms, he hurried off down the hall.

Philip began to smile, but turned to Torgon before it could fully form. "I'm sorry," he began, "perhaps I should have asked your permission first."

"Philip," Torgon clapped him on the shoulder, "I've already given you my permission. Now, perhaps you should go change and catch a breath before dinner. You really need to pull yourself together."

Philip felt dazed as he made his way down the hall toward his suites. He left Torgon to explain the situation to Anna.

5

Nominations

Blasted human woman! Hiro chided either himself or Anna in his head most of the way back to the Rock Clouds. *How could she send for me just to tell me that she's going to be married and leave me alone forever?*

He wasn't actually mad at Anna. He didn't think he'd ever be angry, truly angry, at her ever again. He hated the situation. Hated what he must endure. That didn't help his feelings toward humans, especially King Philip.

He landed on the edge of Rakgar's lair. The Watch hadn't bothered him as he entered the Rock Clouds. No one stopped him, but they didn't seem to care for his presence. Perhaps he had angered them more than he realized when he left home.

Despite the cold reception, Hiro marched into the lair of their leader with purpose. His claws clacked against the hard, stone surface as he tried to forget the pain of Anna's comments and focus on what he had come to report.

When he reached the interior cavern, he saw Rakgar shadowed by his new minions, Milah and Mitashio. Their sneers and eyerolls were the only acknowledgement of Hiro's appearance. Two other large dans, one gray with black spots on his head and tail, the other gray with brown feet, dipped their heads to Hiro. He didn't know their names.

"Shining days, Rakgar." Hiro stepped forward into the circle of sun cast by the distant crevice in the rock above. "I have something to report of my venture to the surface."

Rakgar's eyes wandered to Hiro as he entered, but now his lip twitched as a notion of anger swept his face. He smoothed it a moment later. Hiro couldn't blame him for his anger. He knew he hadn't exactly been the easiest dragon to live with of late. "Yes, Hiro? What is it?"

"A memory," Hiro answered. He stepped in front of Rakgar. Placing his nose close to Rakgar's, he recalled the horrible image and breathed into his face.

Rakgar's eyes glazed over momentarily. As they did, Hiro recalled with perfect clarity what he had seen. Upon his journey back from Kingstor Noble, he flew north of the Black Forest to avoid it. He ended up taking his time coming home and, following his route, he drifted further and further north. Closer to the Courageous Kingdom, he saw it.

The horizon was filled with low, pointed structures in neat little rows. The scene reminded Hiro of the little plants beginning to sprout in Jarek's fields, except they were all brown. Line upon line of little structures. Behind the smaller structures in his line of sight, further north, were bigger ones. Also brown, banners and flags decorated them in gold. Several points reached from the tops of the larger structures. Upon circling through the air around these bigger mysteries, he discovered humans sliding in and out of several of them.

He drifted around them, far enough away that the humans couldn't do anything about his presence. Several humans came out of the little hovels. They reminded Hiro of the dwellings the centaurs used as they travelled. Anna had called them "tents" when they saw a similar sight. An army. The humans wandering into and around them wore the gold tunics of the Courageous Kingdom with a black sword emblazoned on the front and a black sword worn at their hip.

"They're gathering," Hiro said as Rakgar's eyes cleared only moments after he'd received the memory. "Not far from here."

"Who?" Mitashio asked.

"Humans," Hiro answered before Rakgar could cut him off.

Milah and Mitashio looked at each other with furrowed brows but waited until their leader turned his nose to give them the same memory. Rakgar then turned to the other side to give the same memory to two other dragons Hiro didn't recognize.

"Something must be done, Rakgar," the gray and black dragon said after the memory ceased.

"Such as?" Rakgar asked in his deep tone.

"Attack them before they attack us." Hiro's voice was low, but everyone heard it.

Rakgar shook his head. "A planned attack? A mere animal would never do such a thing."

In the silence, Hiro ground his teeth together. How could Rakgar stand to do nothing in the face of such a threat?

"Perhaps," it was the gray and brown dragon speaking this time, "it doesn't have to be organized."

"If we sent a large group of females," Milah voiced, eliciting wide eyes from Hiro, "it might seem merely like a hunt." Looking around at the group, Hiro and Milah saw many wide eyes. "Many animals hunt in groups. They could attack the pack animals first, then fight back as the humans defend their animals."

"It would be enough to weaken their army, at least briefly," the gray and black dragon spoke again. "Humans can't travel well without animals to carry them."

So as not to be left out, Mitashio sat up. "Small attacks to the—"

"ENOUGH!" Rakgar roared and silence blossomed in the cave. "Trivall, Hyrshem, I'm disappointed that you would encourage these young ones in such talk."

"We are no longer young ones, Rakgar." Hiro could hear Milah struggling to keep the hatchling whine out of his voice.

"We are all here to consult you, Rakgar," Trivall said, nodding to Milah's words. "And unless I'm much mistaken, we all feel the human threat is growing too large to ignore any longer."

At these words, Rakgar searched the eyes around him.

Before he could answer, the clacking of claws on stone met the ears of the group. Most of them turned to see several dragons running into the cave. Surneen, Tog's mate, led the group of five females, returning early from a hunt. Tog came running in behind the group.

Tog ran around the group to sit next to Hiro. "What are you doing here?" he whispered to Hiro as Surneen greeted Rakgar. "Where have you been?"

"Long story," Hiro whispered back to put him off the last question. "But to answer your first question..." he moved his nose in front of Tog and relayed to him the entire conversation as it had taken place since he came into the cave. He included the memory of the army from the Courageous Kingdom to get him entirely up to speed.

Tog blinked away the memories as Surneen announced, "Rakgar, we have seen a vast human army to the north." She moved to share the memory with Rakgar as Prak galloped into the cavern behind them.

Prak, noticing where Hiro and Tog sat at the front of the crowd, skidded around the group of females to join them.

"What's going on?" he whispered, but it was hardly a whisper the way Prak intoned it. "I didn't know you were back, Hiro. I came to see Tog and ask him if he knew when you would be back. What is the hunting party doing here? Isn't it too soon for them to be back? Will you be staying long, Hiro? Tog, when are you leaving? I was hoping we could…" Prak's urgent whispers trailed off as Rakgar turned his head on the miniscule dragon. Prak sunk his head to the ground and remained silent.

Rakgar shared the memory with Trivall and Milah, who shared it with the dragons on their respective sides away from Rakgar. As the memory spread through the group, Hiro realized Surneen had seen the same army as he had, and probably only moments after.

"An army in the south," Hiro grumbled, "an army in the north, and King Philip to the east. How can you not see this as a threat?"

Rakgar's lip pulled back to bare his fangs. "We don't know why the humans are gathering. They could be going to fight each other."

Hiro felt the urge to pull his own lip back, but tried to remain calm.

"The gold army is traveling south toward the Rock Clouds," Surneen said. "We could easily see their path and surmise the direction. They aren't shifting to the east or west."

"And what will they do when they arrive?" Rakgar sat up straight, glaring down his nose at the opponents surrounding him. "They have no means to get into the Rock Clouds. They can climb up the Inner Mountain all they desire, but it will afford them nothing."

This statement was met with silence. Rakgar visibly relaxed as he again searched the eyes around him, but this time in triumph.

When Rakgar's eyes landed on Hiro, he shook his head. "No, the faeries are helping them."

Milah grimaced at the ground. "We know from the last time Hiro encountered them that the faeries are with the humans."

"Who knows what kind of majikal means they might devise to help the humans attain the Rock Clouds?" Surneen said. Her posture hadn't moved from her seated upright position.

"Could they really make an entire army fly?" Hyrshem muttered.

"They were able to kidnap Priya. Capture me. Capture Hiro!" Tog said. "They're making a dragon poison—"

"That hasn't been proven—" Rakgar snapped.

"—and who can guess what else they're capable of," Tog growled.

Silence once again echoed through the cave.

"Something must be done, Rakgar," Hiro said.

"He's right," Surneen said, and graced Hiro with a nod.

"I hate to say it," Milah almost whispered, "but I agree."

Rakgar snorted at him. "Fine. You want to do something about it?" He was answered with stern nods and glares. "I'll send three of you to the top of the Inner Mountain. There you will consult with Visi and see what can and should be done."

"Visi?" Tog questioned. "Why should we go see her?"

"She'll have answers, Toggil," Milah said, then taking a step toward Rakgar, he offered, "I'll go. I'll take whatever guidance she can give and bring it straight back to you, Rakgar."

Rakgar nodded, "I think Hiro should go as well. He seems to be the one who continues to have run-ins with the humans."

"I'll go with him," Tog said from Hiro's side. "If only to break up fights between the two of you."

Hiro gave Tog a half-grin as Prak began to bounce at his side. "Rakgar," he whispered, "Rakgar, can I please go, too?" His voice grew louder as one by one the dragons noticed him again. "I promise I won't get in the way. I'll do whatever you need me to do. I'll carry messages, gather food, carry food if I have to, I'll—"

"Prakyndar," Rakgar grinned, "you are also a fully accepted member of this ruck. I can't prevent you from traveling to see Visi whenever you want."

6

Opine

"Sire," Murthur said from his post by the door, "you'll wear a hole in the floor."

Philip slowed his pacing across his apartments to glare at Murthur. "You know very well I won't."

Murthur had relieved his brother Ruther before the king had to dress for dinner. Philip thought briefly how the younger of the two had taken offense at Philip's opinion about his attire for the announcement that day.

"Perhaps you could stroll through the gardens, Your Majesty," Murthur suggested. It wasn't the first time he had suggested walking off his anxiety and it would keep Philip's mind from the upcoming dinner.

Philip shook his head. "I don't want anyone to see me so agitated. Father said the kingdom should always see me at my best. I can only look and act how I really feel within the confines of my chambers."

Murthur nodded, "You are a wise man to remember and adhere to good advice."

Philip stopped in the middle of his sleeping chamber. "Speaking of advice," he said, "what should I say to her?"

Murthur blinked. "To Tierni?"

Philip sat down in one of the chairs in front of his desk. Placing his face in his hands, he muttered, "What was I thinking, inviting her to dinner? I have no idea what to say or do around her." He looked up at his servant. "I can't even think straight while I'm looking into her eyes."

Murthur's face broke into a smile. "I know the feeling well, Your Majesty."

"You do?" Philip asked. Then, checking the servant's wrist, he saw the thin blue ribbon around it. "But you've been married for several years. Why would you be nervous around your wife?"

Murthur took a step closer to Philip. "I remember the nerve-wracking feeling, before we married, of wanting to talk to her, but not knowing what to say. I said many stupid things before I could even put a full sentence together around her. She always giggled and smiled and that just made me feel more a fool. Eventually, whenever she was around I would say very little. She finally asked me to speak up with her and I confessed that I didn't know what to say. My advice would be to keep your mouth shut as much as possible until you can think more clearly when she's around you. Let her speak. That's the best way to get to know her."

Philip nodded. "I can do that."

Murthur stepped to the door to swing it open. "Then I believe we should head to the dining hall before the others think you're not coming."

When king and servant entered the dining hall a few minutes later, everyone else was already in their seats, including Tierni. As ceremony dictated, everyone stood for the king when he entered. Awkwardly, they remained silent.

Since Dieko wasn't there, Anna took his place on Philip's right side. She nodded and smiled as Philip passed her on the way to his spot at the head of the table. Her smile seemed more genuine than Philip had ever seen it. Perhaps she felt for his situation with Tierni. Or found humor in it.

Because of his title and their relationship, Torgon could choose the side on which to sit next to Philip. As the royal general, and one unwilling to attain the throne, ceremony would dictate the left side, and that was the side he had taken. However, unceremoniously, he had allowed Tierni to sit in the first seat closest to Philip's left.

Before Murthur could slide his chair under his knees, Philip risked a glance at Tierni. The moment he did, he regretted it. Her dark hair fell down around her shoulders as he had seen it once before, but tonight she wore a dark green dress that covered her shoulders. Philip's eyes began to water from the strain of keeping them fixed on her face, instead of on the exposed skin at her neckline. Until his eyes met hers.

Her blue eyes caught his and secured them as surely as his arrows finding their target. When she smiled at him he couldn't help but grin back.

"Thank you for joining us this evening, Tierni," he whispered.

Tierni's eyes glanced quickly at Anna before she answered. "Thank you for inviting me."

Once Tierni took her eyes away, Philip felt a physical release of his muscles that allowed him to sit down. Everyone else also seated themselves.

As Murthur placed Philip's napkin, the young king searched for something to say to start the conversation.

Graciously, Anna began without him. "Tierni was just congratulating me on my wedding announcement."

"Yes," Tierni's voice was smooth and steady. Philip had a hard time believing she hadn't had training as a noblewoman. "I was asking if Lord Dieko would be joining us as well. I would love to meet him."

Soup was being ladled into her bowl and Anna shook her head. "No, I'm sorry, Tierni. Dieko has business to attend. Perhaps you will meet him another day, as I'm sure this won't be your last visit with us. You look lovely in that gown, by the way. Green is a wonderful color on you."

"Thank you, Princess," Tierni said, "and thank you for allowing me to use it."

"You lent her a dress?" Philip asked Anna before he could stop himself. He didn't know what else to say.

"Of course I did," Anna answered between sips of her soup. "She wouldn't rightfully own a gown fit for dining with the king, now would she?"

"So," Philip looked between the two women, "have you two met before? Did you already know each other?"

"I told you, Philip," Anna said, laying aside her spoon, "I know several of the house maids and masters. I met Tierni when I came looking for a new handmaid, when my first one disappeared."

"I remember the day you came," Tierni said. "You chose Amythyst because you claimed it 'seemed like she had a strong constitution', isn't that how you phrased it?"

Anna smiled. "Something like that," she said, "but honestly, it didn't seem like it mattered much at the time. I was going to train whomever I could to fill the role anyway. Although it's too bad I didn't choose you, or else we might have had this dinner together a lot sooner."

The two women smiled at Philip, who turned to Torgon. Torgon gulped a bite of soup so large Philip was surprised he didn't just pick up the bowl and drink from it. Philip turned back to his soup, wishing he could drown in it.

"To be fair," Anna said, "Amythyst has served me very well. The three of us must have lunch again soon."

"Again?" Philip asked, without thinking. He could have hit himself with his spoon for the second time he hadn't stopped himself from blurting out. Glancing at Torgon he could see him shaking his head.

"Yes, again, Philip," Anna said. "I will occasionally have lunch with the kitchen staff, the laundry staff, and whomever else I please. They are all amazing people and have such fascinating lives."

"I doubt you'll get away with that once you're married," Torgon muttered.

Silence.

Anna picked up her water glass. "No," she said, "I suppose I won't."

"Or your trips into the forest," Philip needled her. He didn't want the spotlight on himself, so he tried to keep it on his sister.

Anna waved the idea away. "The life of a married woman will be different in many ways, I'm sure."

Philip relaxed slightly. "At least you'll have a husband to protect and care for you. I often feel inadequate to the task."

"Why should any man be tasked with protecting a woman?" Tierni asked quietly into her soup.

"Exactly to my point, Tierni," Anna said.

"Wait," Torgon leaned on the table toward Tierni when his bowl was removed. "It's a man's job to protect women so they can rear children."

"Don't lean on the table during the meal, Torgon," Tierni said firmly.

Torgon abruptly removed his elbow from the table, allowing a full plate to be placed in front of him. Watching the brief exchange, Philip raised an eyebrow.

This form of etiquette couldn't be as new to Tierni as he thought her station in the castle would have required.

"And why shouldn't a woman know how to protect herself?" Anna asked no one but the room in general.

"Why would a woman have any need to protect herself with a man to watch over her?" Torgon asked. "From whom? From what?"

Anna ignored Torgon's remarks and folded her hands in her lap. "Philip, you are always so concerned for my welfare when I leave the castle. What is it you're afraid of?"

Philip's brows creased in thought. What was it he was afraid could happen to her? "Dragons," he said, "wild animals. Getting thrown from your horse. Breaking your ankle on dismount. Many dangerous things could befall you."

"All of which a well-trained maid or friend by my side could help me in case of," she said as she waved to Tierni, who nodded. "Except a dragon, of course. Even the best swordsman in the kingdom hides behind a rock when a dragon is nearby. No, the most terrifying thing to threaten a woman wandering alone ... is a man!"

"What do you mean?" Torgon asked between bites. "You can't believe that taking Philip or me out into the forest with you would be dangerous."

"Of course not," Anna said, her food all but forgotten. "Other men. Strangers. Let me put it to you this way. Philip," she said turning back to him, "your great-grandfather outlawed women in the army or military because he believed it was the men's job to protect the women. I understand that. Women in general understand that and thank him for his noble efforts. But even though you, as the king of the Noble Kingdom, possess the Noble Sword and feel its majikal effect, doesn't mean that every other man in the kingdom does as well."

"Now that's difficult to believe," Philip waved his fork at her after taking a bite. "Everyone knows and feels the effect of the kingdom's sword in which they live. The faeries made sure of that in their enchantment of the swords."

"Yes, Philip," Anna said, "everyone feels the effect, but they don't always act on it. Not every man in the Noble Kingdom acts from the given nobility they share with the kingdom's sword. Even if they do, they might only feel superior, and not behave with nobility. In other words, not for the benefit of the kingdom, but as if they can do whatever they want."

"Now that's a question of the definition of nobility," Philip said. He'd had this debate with his father many times. "Many people have a different definition of what it means to be noble."

"Therefore," Anna stated, "people can feel a different effect of the sword, according to their belief."

Philip looked at Torgon, who rolled his eyes, so the king turned back to Anna. "Really, Anna, I believe this is a discussion for more scholarly minds."

"Well, then," Tierni spoke, laying aside her fork, "let me explain it to you."

Philip turned to her with a grin, enjoying any reason to stare into those eyes. Anna picked up her fork to focus on her food and Philip gestured for Tierni to continue.

"Just the other day I went to the market in town. I needed several things, so I had my basket with me. I needed some cloth and buttons to make my mother a birthday gift. I stopped at a small cart that had some pieces I was interested in."

"While I was searching the cart, I noticed a man sitting across the street, on a bench. I remember he had a red cloth tied around his leg, just above his left knee. He didn't seem unruly. He was just resting; he might have been waiting for someone. He caught my eye and nodded his head and tipped his hat. I nodded back and didn't think much of it.

"I couldn't find what I wanted, so I left the cart and walked along to a shop, but the shop was closed. As I was looking at the sign in the window, I saw the man from the bench in the reflection, shuffling up the street behind me. His head was down, but I knew it was him from the red cloth around his knee. He was walking straight toward me.

"I didn't know what he could want, so I avoided him, and I hurried further on to a shop where I knew I could find buttons. I stepped inside before he might see me. I turned and peeked out the window up the street, hoping I was just being paranoid. But the man was headed directly toward the shop where I was watching from the window.

"That's when I panicked. I didn't know this man. He didn't look cruel, but he was a large man, much larger than the shop owner and me put together. I didn't know what to do. I slipped behind the rack of buttons right before he came in the door.

"When he came inside, the shop owner offered assistance, but he just grunted, stepped back outside, and disappeared. I waited a moment to gather my thoughts, but my shopping was forgotten. I could only take a few deep breaths and leave the shop.

"I didn't see him anywhere and I began to relax, but then he stepped out in front of me from the door of the next shop. I quickly turned back the other way before we could make eye contact, and hurried to turn into a side street.

"I wanted to lose him so I twisted my way through the streets, but I couldn't think straight. I could only think of getting away. I turned too many times and before I knew it, I was lost in a dead-end alleyway. I turned to go back out, but suddenly he was there in front of me again, blocking my escape."

Philip ignored the loud bang he heard from somewhere. "I'll have his head," he whispered.

"Not if I get it first," Torgon growled.

"Gentlemen!" Anna shouted. Philip tore his eyes from Tierni to look down at Anna. She stared up at him in wonder. "You can't protect her after the fact."

Philip's gaze moved from Anna to Tierni, and then to Torgon. When their eyes met, both young men realized they'd jumped to their feet. Murthur struggled behind the king to right his chair.

Tierni turned her full attention on Philip. "I'm sorry if I upset Your Majesty, but as it was, the man didn't mean any harm."

Philip released a breath. He let Murthur help him with his chair. Once he was seated again, he asked, "What happened? What did he do?"

"He handed me a piece of cloth," she said, shrugging. "He thought I had dropped it when I was at the first cart, and he was trying to return it to me. I didn't know what to do. I just stood there. He said little, I don't even remember what he said. I just remember his look of horror when he realized how the fear on my face would look to anyone who wandered by." Tierni shook her head as it hung over her plate. "He left the cloth with me, hobbled away as fast as his legs could take him, and I've never seen him since."

"But he did you no harm?" Torgon asked.

"No," Tierni answered, "but the point is, you wouldn't have been there to protect me if he had."

Philip stared at his half-eaten food, not seeing it. "What do you propose, Anna?"

"Teach them."

Philip looked up at her. "Teach who, what?"

Anna leaned forward. "Teach women to protect themselves. Allow them to wield a sword and fight for themselves."

"They've never been forbidden from doing so," Philip said.

"No," Anna agreed, "but the army is the only place any real training is done. And women are not allowed in the army."

Philip resisted the urge to scratch his head while he thought. "That would be a drastic change, to allow women in the army."

"You don't have to allow women in the army," Anna said. "Just teach them how to fight."

"Any of my men would take it as an insult to be given such a duty, whether it was meant that way or not." He added the last at Anna's pursed lips.

"Torgon," Tierni said, "you've taught me a few things to do to protect myself."

"With father's help," Torgon corrected.

"But you would be a wonderful teacher to others as well, I'm sure," Tierni insisted.

"I would do it, yes, but..." Torgon's voice trailed off as he looked to Philip for assistance.

Philip could sense his dilemma and chimed in. "He has far too many duties both here in the castle and training the men for me to add more."

They all sat in silence for a moment. Philip longed to change the conversation from this issue and searched his mind for something else to talk about as he reached for his fork again.

"I'll teach them," Anna said suddenly.

"What?" Torgon exclaimed.

"You?" Philip asked. "How will you teach them?"

"Sar taught me the sword," she said. "It would be easy enough."

Tierni nodded enthusiastically. Philip turned to her. "You would be willing to learn from my sister?"

"Of course I would!" Tierni said.

Philip looked to Torgon for advice. Torgon picked up his wine glass and shrugged.

Philip sighed, "Do as you wish, ladies, but be prepared for the difficulty of it." As he watched both women smile and discuss plans for meeting times and places, his gaze rested on Tierni, but his mind dwelt on Anna. She could wield a sword? What else did he not know of her? How many more secrets did he need to discover?

7

The One

It had only been three days, but Hiro could barely lift another claw. They had stuffed themselves full of lydik and even part of a scorrand before their journey, but the four dragons stumbled with weak fire as they fought their way up the Inner Mountain. Partway up their ascent, late in the second sun cycle, they found a herd of stringy, gray beasts with horns. Each was only a couple of mouthfuls, and they ate as many as they could. But their fires still waned.

Hiro was surprised to discover that the fire in his belly didn't gutter as often as he thought it would while they traveled. He thought this journey would be as good as a death sentence for him. But as he followed the others over the rise to see Visi's cavern lair opening ahead of them, his fire burned hot and bright deep within him.

Milah had tried to take the lead early on, but Hiro wouldn't have it. Although each dragon had received the memory of how to get to the old seer dame, Milah assumed himself as the leader of the group in Rakgar's stead. When he tried to tell Hiro what to do, Hiro dug in his claws and did everything the exact opposite.

Tog turned the table on Milah and fell in line behind Hiro, assuming that if he and Prak followed Hiro, Milah would be forced to follow him too, but Milah proved as impossible to lead as Hiro. Eventually, Tog suggested they treat the expedition as four dragons travelling toward the same goal. Then Prak naturally took the lead for the rest of the journey.

However, flying up the mountain had proved almost impossible. Something in the air pulled the dragons toward the ground with so much strength that they spent more energy trying to get lift than they would have spent climbing the rock. They assumed the energy was a variant of the same force that kept the mountains floating. Halfway through the first sun cycle, they agreed to walk, which was the first and only thing they ever eventually agreed upon. Toward sunset the same day, talking nearly ceased. Even for Prak.

"Not much further," Prak said over his back to the others. Prak had the most strength of anyone in the group, but his head drooped as low as the rest of theirs.

Digging in his claws, Hiro added his own gouges to the rock under him as many others had before. The mountain was sparse of life so close to the summit. At the bottom there had been trees and lakes. Toward the middle of the mountain short bushes dotted the hillsides and creeks ran clear and bubbling. Now, toward the top, not even grass grew. They'd left that behind in the middle of the day. The foreboding rock landscape warned them not to go any further. Summer wasn't a distant memory up here; it had simply never existed.

As the four crawled over the rocks toward Visi's lair opening, Tog whispered, "What do we do if she's not here?"

They all paused, shoulders slumping, legs shaking, tails dragging. Hiro looked at Milah; Tog looked at Prak.

"She'll be here," Prak muttered, without much hope in his voice.

Milah's legs tentatively stepped over small boulders scattered around the opening. When Hiro crawled up beside him, his head tilted toward Hiro. "Do you think she knows we're coming?" he whispered.

"Of course she knows!" A voice like rocks grinding together called out to them from inside. Four dragon heads lifted at the sound of her voice. Not because it was familiar or welcoming, but because it was present.

Prak was the first to reach the old dame. "I knew you would be here," he said with what little breath he had left.

"Always the optimist, little one," Visi replied. "Inside," she directed him and the others. "I have a wonderful little herb to lift you."

The old dragon dame was exactly as Hiro remembered her. Her once glorious white scales, now dirty and dull. The hide around her joints and eyes, slack and missing scales.

Inside the cave, Hiro smelled flesh and leaf, dirt and flower, fire of dragon and fire of human, all at the same time. It smelled like Priya. The cave was lit with glowing rocks and fires on sticks, in clumps of firewood, or burning in large metal cauldrons in multiple hues. The mere fact that Hiro noticed the scents and light before the warmth spoke volumes because the heat was stifling, even for a dragon.

Once inside, Visi motioned with her front claw to the large empty space against the wall. "Sit, rest," she said, but she turned to gather some brown twigs from a pile amidst numerous plants of all varieties against the opposite wall.

The front cavern was just large enough for the five dragons to lie down and rest. Three large cloths hung against the wall. All three were a dirty brown color and decorated with what looked like charcoal markings, none of which could be deciphered. One of them billowed into a darkened opening beyond, so Hiro assumed all three cloths covered secret escapes.

"Here," she said, placing a gnarled branch in front of each dragon as they slumped onto the ground. "Eat these, they'll give you a little strength."

"Thank you," Prak said as she placed one in front of him.

Hiro glanced at Tog, who was inspecting the little stick. He met Hiro's gaze with one eye and shrugged his shoulder. Hiro rolled his shoulder, then licked the crunchy brown twig from the ground. It crumpled in his mouth and slid down his throat before he could even taste it.

"What is it?" Milah asked as he sniffed at it.

"Dried pixie root," Visi answered. "It should reawaken your faculties long enough for you to get back down the mountain."

Once they had all eaten the root, Milah spoke up. "We came from Rakgar on urgent business. We need answers."

Visi glared at Milah. "Rakgar," she sneered the title, "only sends anyone to me if he wants to waste their time." She turned her drooping eyes on Hiro. "Anyone else comes of their own accord."

"Do you know why we're here?" Hiro asked.

"Yes," she said.

"Please, Visi," Prak spoke up, "the dragons are in danger. We need help. We need to know what we can do. Can you give us any advice? Can you give us any guidance at all?"

"Now you," she said to Prak with a smile, "you came of your own accord, didn't you, little one?"

"I did," Prak said sitting up a little straighter.

"And your questions, I will answer," she told him.

"Hang on," Milah spoke up. They all sat up straighter and with more fire in their eyes as the root herb began working. "We all traveled here of our own free will. We could have refused to come."

Visi's eyes slid to Milah. She nodded slowly. "Indeed, young one. But I am not a hired shaman to give answers at Rakgar's beckon. I give answers to those I deem worthy."

"And are we?" Tog asked. "Worthy, I mean?"

Visi's eyebrows dropped. "Yes," she said, "yes, I believe you are." She turned to Milah. "All of you."

The four waited in silence. Visi walked slowly before the four dragons, staring each of them in the eye as she passed. Finally, she stopped in front of Milah. "Milah, you will amount to nothing. Your ambition and talents will be utterly wasted." Milah's maw dropped. "Unless..." Milah's jaw snapped shut, his eyes bright with anticipation, "...you listen to your betters. In this case—"

Milah began growling, but Visi continued. "I was not going to say Hiro—"

"Thank Shurta!" Milah stared up into the ceiling of the cave.

"On the contrary," Visi continued, "I was going to say Prakyndar."

"What?!" Milah leaped to his feet. "You can't be serious! What does that sniveling worm have to teach me?"

Visi sighed, rolling her eyes. "Manners, for one."

Milah reseated himself, grumbling under his breath. Hiro caught words like "useless" and "worm," and something about someone being right.

Visi stepped from Milah to Prak. "Prak, don't shirk the name. You will be a thorn in the side of your enemies and you will be a great leader." Milah groaned, but Visi ignored him. "Remember," she told the small brown dragon, "to stand up for what you believe to be right. Don't let anyone else sway you, and you will change the world."

Prak smiled at Hiro, and Hiro nodded his head to the little dragon as Visi stopped in front of Tog.

"I'm sorry to tell you this, Toggil," she said, her aged eyes burning behind tears, "you, who have always tried to follow the rules. Your rules will force you to abandon your closest friend in the world in his greatest time of need."

Tog's face fell. Prak shrank back a little. Even Milah turned in shock. "I would never do that," Tog whispered.

"Nevertheless," she whispered back not unkindly, "abandon him you shall. Unless you learn to think for yourself and set aside what you have been taught to be right, you will lose him forever. As will the world."

With this revelation, she turned to look at Hiro. Her white eyes bore into his. "Hiro feira Dakoon," she whispered. "You are The One."

Hiro felt a wave of ice wash over him. In the back of his mind, he wondered where all the warmth in the cave had gone. He stared into Visi's eyes. All the time he had hated the name Dakoon and hoped to change it held much more meaning now. The old seer dame had been the one to name him. Had she named him Dakoon at his birth because she knew then that he was The One?

The legend of The One, the one who would bring dragons and humans together "in ways unimaginable," had been passed around every dragon and every ruck for as long as dragons could speak.

However, dragons no longer wanted the story of The One to be true. They didn't want to be united with humans, in any way! Could this union have something to do with his relationship with Anna?

When Hiro's mind turned to Anna, his fire guttered again. This time his heat constricted so much that Hiro felt a sharp pain surrounding the other half of his heart still in his chest. He grimaced as his insides pulsed in icy pain. Turning away from Visi, he belched a flame. When he looked back to her, she nodded. "It begins," she said.

"What begins?" Prak asked. "What's going on? Is there something you can do for Hiro? Do you know what's happening to him?"

Visi turned and walked toward the far cloth hanging against the wall. She pushed her head and withers through it, then turned back to face Hiro. "Come with me," she said, "we need to talk. Privately."

Hiro glid through the curtained off section of the cave. The next room was darker, although several glowing rocks floated at the top of the cavern. A pile of rumpled cloths lay bunched in a corner of the cave, which reminded Hiro of his bed of grasses. Next to it, a small pile of shining, gold trinkets were stacked against the wall. Visi walked into the middle of the space, then, turning as Hiro entered, she sat up straight and tall on her back haunches.

The second cave wasn't large. There might have been enough room for three dragons inside it. Entering the tight space, Hiro didn't want to crowd Visi, so he hung back away from her.

"Bring your tail through," she said, indicating his hind end. He wrapped his tail around his body to get it inside from under the cloth. Once the cloth hung loose again, she looked him in the eye. "The markings on the cloth will keep us from being heard only when it hangs freely."

Hiro nodded, taking note not to disturb the hanging behind him.

Visi stared him in the eye for an uncomfortable amount of time. Finally, she nodded once. "You are not The One," she said.

Hiro's brow creased. "But you said—"

"Exactly what the others needed to hear," she answered abruptly. "However, you are one half of The One, each manipulated by the other."

Hiro blinked. He hadn't yet figured out whether he was happy or sad about being The One and now suddenly, he wasn't The One anymore but only half! "I don't understand," he said.

"Of course not," Visi grinned, "because you don't take the time to understand."

What she said tickled the back of Hiro's mind, but he couldn't think clearly. "Dragons are not manipulated by anyone," he said.

"Really?" Visi mocked him. "Is not a dan moved by the dame he loves?"

"My heart?" he asked. "You can't mean to say...?" His voice trailed off, because he didn't know how much Visi knew about Anna.

As soon as he thought of her, his fire spluttered dangerously close to extinguishing. He coughed up more fire, spitting and hacking flame, but cold compressed his heart and insides the whole while. He belched a long flame, avoiding the bed of cloths and the hanging on the wall, but only just. When he could produce no more, he slumped onto the ground. As the fire in his belly flickered to life, he gazed up at Visi. "Am I dying?" he asked.

Visi tilted her head, but nothing in her eyes showed compassion. "You are being forged," she said. "You are the tip of a sword, but a sword cannot be used in combat without a hilt and handle. Hiro, you are one half of a whole that creates something formidable. Be mindful who wields you."

8

Hindrance

Weak and shocked, Hiro allowed himself and the others to be unceremoniously dismissed from Visi's cave. "Get out of my sight!" is the phrase he thought he heard through the clamor. Milah and Prak protested quite loudly. While Milah's protests were harshly answered or ignored altogether, Prak's was at least met with a brief explanation, but Hiro only grasped a little of it as they were forced from the old seer's lair. The four dans were sent on their way with only small fires in their bellies and no useful guidance to deliver to Rakgar.

The return trip down the mountain wasn't as difficult as the way up, although Hiro's fire fought him more than the cold, thin air. The four were able to fly down the mountain and slip silently past the increasingly green landscape. But Hiro could only think of Anna, Priya, and the dragons' predicament. However, he soon realized that every time he thought of Anna, his fire would dwindle.

"I've been studying with Rakgar," Milah's growl could be heard drifting back from well ahead of Hiro and Tog. "What could you possibly teach me about war or strategies or anything else?"

"You might be surprised," Prak's nasal voice also reached them. "My father knew the centaurs well. He traveled with them in the Just Kingdom for a while. The humans of the Just Kingdom are strategists. The centaurs would study their stratagem and training. Even the faeries find the Just Kingdom formidable. My father taught me everything they taught him. I know a thing or two."

"That doesn't mean you can apply it," Milah argued. "I've been counseling Rakgar. I've learned a lot too."

"You haven't been counseling him very long," Prak said. "Besides, Rakgar gives dragons assignments. He doesn't command armies. He doesn't know—"

"Exactly," Milah cut him off, "Rakgar is a leader. Your father was never a leader. How can you teach leadership without actually being a leader?"

"My father was a great dan!" Prak nearly screamed. "There has never been a need for him to step up and command an army, but he certainly could have! Besides, I'm friends with centaurs as well!"

Prak put his nose up to Milah, undoubtedly relaying his meeting with the centaurs, but when Milah blinked away the memory, he also shook his head. "That could be anyone's memory. And even if it were true, it doesn't necessarily make you a good leader." Milah drifted back toward Hiro and Tog on a cool current. "Hiro, Tog," he called, "does this worm actually know any centaur leaders?"

Both Tog and Hiro only glared at him until he flew ahead of them again to continue his argument with Prak.

Once the intensity of the two other dragons' voices quieted due to the distance between them, Tog asked, "Hiro, are you alright?"

"I'm fine," Hiro mumbled back. What could he say to Tog at this point?

"Is your fire still bothering you?" he asked quietly.

Hiro sensed Tog's discomfort after leaving their conversation with the old dame. He rolled a shoulder. "It's getting better," he lied. "I think I can at least predict when it's going to happen now."

"You know," Tog said as they skirted some extra tall trees, "I don't think Visi is always right."

Hiro inspected his best friend at these words. When their eyes met, Hiro could clearly see Tog's eyes were wet around the edges. He must have taken Visi's warning seriously. "What do you mean?" Hiro asked.

Tog glanced sidelong at Hiro. "I mean she couldn't possibly be right." He gave his head a small shake and the moisture in his eyes disappeared. "I would never abandon you, Hiro." Tog turned his head and both his toggling eyes stared into Hiro's. "Never."

Hiro nodded at Tog. Tog nodded back, and they flew on in silence.

"Shall we?"

Torgon swept his arm into a deep, overly formal bow, "After you, My Liege."

Philip tried in vain to keep the grin off his face. "Whatever happens," he said over his shoulder to Torgon as he stepped through the door to the outdoor training grounds behind the castle, "we must try to at least look supportive."

"I am fully supportive," Torgon said while following his friend. "I'll support my sister's fancy until she wakes up and realizes it's a folly. I always have."

Backs straight and hands resting on pommels, the two young men walked out into the summer sunshine. It was a perfect, bright day, but Philip couldn't enjoy it long because he knew the sweat would be rolling sooner rather than later. They walked to the open-air grounds to exchange their embroidered and gilded vests and tunics for heavy chainmail and thickly padded training vests. As Philip removed his vest, Torgon nudged him in the ribs. Catching his eye, Torgon jerked his head toward a far-off section of the training grounds.

The men already training had moved away from a shaded area next to the woods. It was a section often sought after for training in the summer, other than the shaded open space under the castle. Nobility has its privileges and the two areas were often given to the higher ranks and royalty.

However, training today in this section were four women. Anna, Tierni, and two other women whom Philip didn't recognize. The third and fourth women were both larger than Anna and Tierni.

Although taller, one could still barely lift a sword, so she swung a large stick, attempting to imitate the men's large circles. Unfortunately, she repeatedly caught herself on the elbow or shoulder, eliciting chuckles from nearby.

But the last woman could have lifted a horse! With Anna's encouragement, she swung what Philip hoped was a blunted sword in smooth circles, but she seemed hesitant to shift its momentum. Philip tried hard not to wince as Tierni lifted one of the heavy, broad swords over her head only to have it topple behind her. When she tried to catch herself, her skirt lifted higher than her knees in back, flashing her undergarments. Philip willed himself not to blush as he hastily turned away.

Most of the men only partly paid attention to their own training, half-heartedly swinging their swords in half and full figure-eights. Some men blatantly leaned on their swords to watch the women. Philip could hear a few whispered comments behind hands, but what he noticed the most were the men's smiles. Every man wore a smile on his face. Whether it was a mocking smile or an incredulous smile, the arrogant grins surrounded him.

When Tierni tried to lift the sword again, one of the men leaning on his sword nearby laughed aloud when she toppled over.

"This has gone on long enough," Philip said. Grinding his teeth, he marched toward the women.

"Are you going to stop them?" Torgon asked, running to catch up.

"Of course not," Philip growled back at him, "but the men's behavior only proves what they told us at dinner."

As he approached the women, all four of them slowed their weapons, turning to the king. The men who had been watching them plucked their swords into their hands and hastily wiped their brows as if they had been hard at work.

"Good morning, Anna," Philip said, nodding as he approached. But once he got to the edge of the field that separated the women's practice area from the men's, he turned his back to the women. "Gentlemen," he said loud enough for everyone to hear, "I see that you have noticed our newest practice companions. I want everyone to know that I fully support my sister, Anna, and anyone she wishes to train. I also want to warn you that anyone who denigrates these women in their quest to protect themselves will personally answer to me."

The grins dropped from the men's faces. As they returned to their practice, Philip glared them down.

"Thank you, Philip," Anna said behind him. "I'm sure that will help tremendously."

Philip turned to face her, steeling himself. "Are you sure you want to do this, Anna?" he asked. "I can only do so much to control the actions of my men. It's not going to be easy."

"I know," she answered.

"We all know," Tierni added behind her.

"And we appreciate what you are willing to do," Anna finished. "We're prepared for the rest."

Philip took a breath, ready to argue about the difficulties they would face, but before he could say more, Torgon grabbed his arm. "Faerie," he whispered in his ear.

All thought of Anna and her ladies fled his mind as Philip turned to look back at the castle. In the warm, open air of the practice field the faerie drifted on wing toward the king and his general. His cloak billowed under him as he landed on the soft grass in front of the two men.

Qialla inclined his head. "A message from the Courageous Kingdom, Sire." He pulled a folded parchment from under his cloak to pass to Philip.

Philip only just kept his brow from pinching together in a scowl. "Why would our guest be delivering a message?" he asked, hoping his voice sounded curious instead of angry. "That's the duty of the royal messengers."

"These matters," Qialla dipped his head again, "are too important to be left to younglings."

Younglings. *I'm a youngling in your eyes,* Philip thought to himself as he inspected the seal. Undoubtedly, it was the seal from King Torodov and it appeared unbroken. *But,* Philip thought, *faeries could use some kind of majik to reseal it, I'm sure.*

He shared a glance with Torgon, who inspected the parchment over Philip's shoulder. The look on his face made Philip think his general might be considering the same thought. Without speaking their concerns, Philip broke the seal and unfolded the parchment.

For the eyes of King Philip
with the Noble Sword at His Side
From the hand of King Torodov
with the Courageous Sword at His Side

A messenger has been sent to
deliver a formal voice of apology.
That correspondence will follow.
Do with the Voice of the Message
as you see fit.

For now, this means of note must
suffice. The Courageous Army will
arrive at the base of the
Inner Mountain in one week's
time. There, we shall await
your command.

-Your Servant

Philip remained expressionless as he looked up from the letter into Qialla's dark cowl. "The Courageous Kingdom is almost to the Inner Mountain," he told the faerie. "A large part of my army is already on the way and we will leave after my sister's wedding to join them."

"Do you really think it wise to proceed with a wedding and frivolity under such dire circumstances?" Qialla asked with flat emotion.

Philip nodded. "I think it is good to keep up the spirits of my people. They should see that we will remain strong after this trivial war. Besides, should anything happen to me, the wedding ensures that someone will be in line to rule the kingdom."

When the faerie heaved a sigh Philip thought he might have heard a groan behind it, but he brushed it aside. For now, he could use Anna's wedding to put off the less pleasant task of this pointless and violent war.

"And the Honorable Kingdom?" Qialla asked.

"They are already most of the way to the Inner Mountain from the south," Philip answered. "They should arrive within the same week as we do."

Qialla bowed lower, "And we shall join you upon your departure."

Philip forced a smile and a nod. The faerie turned to leave and Philip shared another glance with Torgon. Once the faerie had crossed the entire field and entered the castle, Philip finally turned to Torgon.

"This really is happening, isn't it?" Philip whispered.

Torgon looked around at the training men. Most of them had slowed or stopped to watch the exchange with the faerie. Even Anna, Tierni, and the other women had quieted. With a glance from Torgon, the men resumed their practice. Anna and the women talked quietly amongst themselves as Torgon clapped a hand on Philip's shoulder. "Come and swing swords with me," he said low in Philip's ear. "You'll feel better."

The two young men walked back to the bench of practice swords and gear. They strapped up in silence as Philip contemplated the gathering armies.

"Let's start easy to warm up," Torgon said, swinging a lazy figure-eight. "How about The Snake?"

"The Snake?" Philip moaned. "That's not a warm-up, that's suicide."

Torgon laughed as he swung his sword toward Philip. "You want your mind off things, right?"

Philip barely had time to parry the first blow. His sword clanged on Torgon's, but his feet tangled and he missed the last strike.

"Again," Torgon said with a grin.

Philip ground his teeth. Knowing what was coming this time, he kept his footing through the exchange of combinations, but the swing didn't connect.

"Again," Torgon shouted without even a hint of smile this time.

The third time through, Philip missed the fourth block entirely and received a swipe of Torgon's blunted blade along his arm.

"You just lost your arm," Torgon huffed, leaning on his sword.

"I stand to lose a lot more than my arm," Philip grumbled.

"Fine," Torgon threw one hand in the air, "we can work on The Swan, instead."

"You do realize," Philip panted as he parried over and over, "that three armies are gathering and waiting for my command to wipe out an entire species. I think," he ducked and parried, "only the Courageous Kingdom keeps their army at full strength at all times, but we have almost 8,000 men in our army alone."

"Again," Torgon grumbled when Philip's last block was weak enough for Torgon's sword to hit the king's thigh. "And we're not sending our entire army. That would be reckless."

"True," Philip missed the second block, but continued on to the next. "But even if all three armies sent only 5,000 men, that's 15,000 men against a single ruck of dragons."

"That's not including," Torgon said as he started The Swan again without interruption, "the Just and Allegiant Kingdoms."

"We won't know about them until we arrive at the Inner Mountain," Philip said as he blocked. "But if they send only 5,000 each, that's 25,000 men to wipe out a few hundred dragons."

"The Lion!" Torgon yelled, moving into the complex combination without any respite between.

"Is it even possible to do what the faeries demand?" Philip's voice lifted with the increased clatter of the swords. "Why do they even want this war?" He didn't dare voice the purpose of it with so many ears around. "When will it stop?"

"When you stop it!" Torgon yelled as he swung his sword at Philip.

Philip dropped to the ground to roll out of the way. "What do you mean?" Philip felt the reverberation of both swords when they met.

"You're the king!" Torgon swung and shifted into The Dragon without announcing it. "You command the men! Not the faeries! You choose your path!"

"But I have no choice!" Philip bellowed. He swung his sword arcing over his head, feinting The Scorrand, but ending in The Troll. Torgon's talented reactions brought his sword up to block without blinking an eye. He pushed away Philip's attempt and landed a blow to the king's leg.

He yelled as the blade connected with his knee and he dropped to the grass. But the pain in his knee wasn't what made him stop. Philip bent with his hands on his knee. His thoughts spun. "It's happening too fast. I have no control over any of it."

Torgon stood over his king. "Say it, Philip. What is it you fear?"

"How can we allow this to happen?" Philip rubbed his knee. The throbbing eased, but his heart still burned. "Why can't I stop this? What am I missing?"

When he finally looked up at Torgon, the general held out his hand. Philip took it and allowed Torgon to pull him to his feet. He put some weight on his knee and felt no pain. Torgon clapped him on the shoulder again. "You could take any of an infinite number of paths ..."

Philip nodded, and finished the rest of what he remembered former Royal General Bragon reciting, "...the difficulty lies in making our own path."

9

Inept

Rakgar's laugh echoed through the cavern. Hiro, Tog, Prak, and even Milah stood before him, hanging their heads. Milah had passed the memory of what the seer had said to each dragon. Rakgar had glanced briefly at Hiro after receiving it, but didn't ask what more had been said in private before he burst into laughter, his body shaking. Mitashio looked on, both confused and embarrassed for his brother.

Rakgar settled down as the mirth left him and he looked over the smaller dragons in front of him. "Did you expect anything less?" he asked them.

Milah lifted his head first. "I expected some sort of guidance," he told Rakgar, "not the drivel she spouted."

"She's a crazy old dame," Rakgar chuckled again. "I hoped she would see through her fog of insanity to the dangers around her, but alas…" he shook his head.

Hiro ground his teeth. "Then we'll have to make do without her guidance."

Tog tilted his head toward Hiro. Prak nodded.

Rakgar growled. "What do you mean, Hiro?"

"I mean," Hiro lifted his chin slightly and said, "we'll have to figure this out on our own."

Hiro thought Prak's enthusiastic nods might cause the little dragon to start bouncing across the floor. "We've been through this before," Rakgar grumbled at Hiro as he lay down. "Are you proposing anything different?"

"An army is approaching!" Hiro said, snapping his tail in a frenzy. "Perhaps two. Or more! We can't just sit here and let them live in the shadow of our home!"

"So be it," Rakgar waved a claw. "Go. Prepare for war."

Silence rang in Hiro's ears. Did he hear correct? Was Rakgar finally giving them permission to do something about the human army threat? Hiro glanced at the other dragons. Mitashio looked like a boulder had landed on his head. Tog and Prak perked up. But Milah only watched Rakgar. "We have your permission?" Hiro asked cautiously.

"You have my permission," Rakgar nodded.

Hiro took a step toward the cavern opening. Then another.

As Tog and Prak made to follow him, Rakgar called out. "It will be interesting to see how a mere animal prepares for war, will it not?"

Hiro met Rakgar's eye. The warning was plain for anyone to see or hear.

Before Hiro could decide whether he should leave or not, the sound of wings beating the air and the clatter of claws against the rock met their ears.

"Centaurs!" a striped purple dame ran into the cave, announcing the disruption. "Rakgar, the centaurs are at the base of the Inner Mountain. They're asking to meet."

Rakgar stood, "Why do they want to meet?"

Before the dame could answer, Hiro spoke up. "They will stand with us and fight."

"We are not fighting," Rakgar roared.

"Not even for survival?" Hiro roared back.

Rakgar's scales lifted. He ground his teeth and bared his fangs at Hiro. "I will not dive into a rashly conceived, immediate fight with thousands of humans."

"I will," Hiro growled back before he could think.

"Hiro!" Tog snapped, but Hiro ignored him.

Rakgar growled in the back of his throat. He stepped toward Hiro, but had to lower his head to look him in the eye. Rakgar's tail snapped at the end as he whipped it from side to side. "Are you challenging me?"

Hiro took a step toward Rakgar, not taking his eyes from his leader. They glared at each other, crouched in attack position.

"Hiro!" Tog yelled. Finally, Hiro pried his eyes away from Rakgar. "Let's meet with the centaurs," Tog said, once he had Hiro's attention.

Hiro blinked his eyes to clear his fury with Rakgar. He looked sideways at the purple dame. "Who's down there? Which centaurs?"

The dame, dumbfounded at their behavior, shook her head. "Joss, the leader, and other leaders, it seems. They asked to speak with Rakgar."

Rakgar straightened from his posture. "I will speak with him."

"I'll go with you," Hiro made sure it didn't sound like a request.

Milah growled, but Rakgar held a claw up to forestall him, then forced his features to relax, covering his fangs again. "Anyone may go. I can't control your actions. However, a large group of dragons flying into the centaur camp might look suspicious to humans."

"Well," Hiro said as he loped from the cave, "the good thing is that the humans are still far enough away that they won't see it."

The group thundered through the sky toward the centaur camp. Hiro knew the centaurs would see them coming and be prepared. What he didn't expect was for dozens of centaurs to be gathered in a large opening looking skyward expectantly as the dragons approached. They stood in the formation of a large triangle, with Joss at the head and Ashel and Rylan just behind him. The rest of the large camp stayed to their shelters or their business.

Rakgar, Hiro, Milah, Mitashio, Tog, Prak, the purple dame, and several other dragons that had joined them along the way set down in front of the centaurs. Rakgar stepped forward but didn't say anything. He stared at the centaurs, apparently taking in their weapons and armor.

Joss, his dark horse body nearly covered in swords, knives and quills of arrows, stood glowering at the dragons. Ashel, usually smiling and jovial, watched them with a scowl on her face. Her dark hair was braided behind her head and down along her back. Rylan wore leather bracers and cannon-bone armor, but the only weapon he retained was the shining silver sword on his back. Vikal flanked Ashel and held a long knife unsheathed in his hand. His heavy brow creased over his eyes. Hiro recognized several other centaurs from his previous visits but he didn't know their names. They seemed ready to attack, so Hiro dropped back behind Rakgar.

Joss took a step forward but tilted his head to the side to look around Rakgar. "Well met, Hiro," he said, touching his forehead.

"Shining days to you, Joss," Hiro said, touching his brow, nose bridge, then chest.

"You are Joss?" Rakgar asked. "Leader of the centaurs?"

Joss finally turned to face the immense gray dragon in front of him. "I am," he said, touching his forehead with a slight nod.

"I am Rakgar feira Freeg," he said without the centaur greeting. "I believe you asked to speak with me."

Joss looked at each dragon in turn, then nodded. "We've come to offer our assistance to the dragons," he said, returning Rakgar's gaze. "We have noticed dangerous movements among the humans that we feel threaten our allies, the dragons."

"It is kind of you to offer help," Rakgar said, "but we don't want to endanger centaur lives for what is clearly not a serious threat."

"Rakgar," Hiro spoke up, "we should hear them out."

Rakgar sighed, then waved a claw for Joss to continue.

Joss glanced at Hiro before speaking. "The increase in hostilities between the humans and dragons is a great cause for unease," he said. "But the fact of greatest concern is that three armies are only days away from the Rock Clouds. If nothing is done to stop them, tens of thousands of human men will slaughter the dragons of the Rock Clouds while we watch."

"We are only animals to them," Rakgar said, "we can do little about that. Besides, if we stay in the Rock Clouds, they can't bother us there."

"You can do little," Ashel spoke from Joss's side, "but we can do plenty. These humans threaten our friends. We will not stand by." Vikal nodded behind her.

"The threat is greater than you think." Rylan's smooth voice drifted from beside Joss. "I have a crystal ball of my own," he said, turning to Hiro, "acquired without torture, mind you. And I have seen many things in it."

"A centaur majishun?" Rakgar chuckled. "Since when do you allow such a thing?"

"Since he has no choice," Rylan stifled Rakgar's laughter. "I believe in combating the faeries with their own tools. We have found several large wooden platforms in the forest surrounding the Inner Mountain of the Rock Clouds. Faerie majishuns have the means to make these platforms take flight. I know this because I know the spells they would use. I'm certain they can transport the humans into the Rock Clouds."

Hiro could hear the other dragons rumbling uncertainly. "Is it really possible?" he heard Prak ask. Even Milah and Mitashio were taken aback.

"Not to worry," Joss said, "we have destroyed all the platforms we found."

"But I'm sure they possess more that we haven't found," Rylan interjected.

"What are you proposing?" Rakgar asked, once the murmuring died down.

"Strategic strikes," Ashel said. Hiro could hear the warrior in her tone. "Our army is small, but an arrow can bring down a paquar when it strikes at the heart. We should attack any supplies coming in from the north. Small supply trains are easy to pick off and we'll have groups set up to attack those coming from the Courageous and Honorable Kingdoms, but the poison will be coming from the north."

"Poison?" Milah showed his first real sign of surprise.

"What poison?" the purple dame echoed.

Hiro opened his mouth to answer, but Joss stopped him by calling his name. "Hiro," he said, "let Rylan handle this."

Confused, Hiro nodded to Joss. Joss turned and nodded to Rylan. Rylan took a step toward Rakgar.

"Rakgar," Rylan said, taking a few more measured steps, "have you told the other dragons about the dragon poison?"

Rakgar held his head up straight. "I didn't feel the need to incite panic in my ruck."

Ashel snorted. "Since when do dragons panic?" she muttered.

Rylan stood in front of Rakgar. The centaur stared up at the massive gray dragon without fear. The shining silver sword on his back glistened in the sunlight. "But these," he said, indicating Milah and Mitashio, "seem to be close to you. Why haven't you told them? Warned them?"

Rakgar tilted his head down to look at Rylan. "I don't answer to you."

Rylan crossed his arms over his chest and walked forward. As he did, Rakgar's body moved back from the centaur as if it was being pushed at the chest. Rylan stared at Rakgar. Rakgar stared at Rylan. Suddenly, Rylan jumped toward Rakgar. When he did, everyone watched as Rakgar's body was pushed backward by an unseen force.

Confused, Rakgar righted himself as Rylan turned back and trotted to Joss's side again. As he did so, Rylan made eye contact with Joss, shaking his head.

A shadow moved over Joss's face and he turned to glare at Rakgar.

"I'm sorry, Rakgar," Joss said, "but I'm going to have to ask you to leave."

"What are you talking about?" Rakgar bellowed. "I will not allow you to—"

"Allow?" Ashel yelled. Before Hiro could blink, a blade was in her hand and every other centaur other than Joss and Rylan had drawn a weapon of some sort. Vikal drew a second blade.

Joss threw up an open hand to them. "Neither I nor my people will answer to you," he said as he slowly lowered his hand.

"Then who—" Rakgar grumbled, but he stopped as first Joss's gaze, then every other eye in the clearing, drifted to Hiro.

Hiro remembered Ashel's words the last time they had met. "*You will be at the center of a war between the five kingdoms of Avonoa. You might be what they fight over or for or about, but I know you'll be at the heart of it. Hiro, when the time comes, the centaurs will follow you. Only you.*"

Rakgar growled, baring his teeth first at Hiro, then at the centaurs. Rylan stepped forward. With measured movements, he carefully removed the silver sword from its silver scabbard across his back. As he lifted it to point it at Rakgar, the sun's beam sparked from the edges of the weapon. "This is the Allegiant Sword of the Five Swords of Avonoa," Rylan said. "All who withstand its power are loyal to the owner. You failed."

Everyone's attention descended on Rakgar. He in turn searched every face in the clearing. Mitashio watched with his maw agape. Tog's eyes twitched. Vikal narrowed his further. When Rakgar saw that only confusion, sorrow, and anger surrounding him, he leapt into the sky, unfurled his massive gray wings, and flew away.

"I don't understand," Hiro began, questioning the centaurs as they put away their weapons. But Milah interrupted him.

"How did you come by this sword?" Milah barked. "How do we even know it is the Allegiant Sword? How do we know this wasn't all some sort of trick?"

"We came upon the sword as Queen Sarador and her party traveled to the Noble Kingdom for Philip's coronation," Ashel said. "We weren't going to engage the party, we only meant to watch them to make sure they passed in peace. But when we discovered that they carried with them the real sword and not a duplicate for the ceremonies, well..." she shrugged her shoulders and grinned at Hiro. "Call me a dragon, but I just can't resist something shiny."

"Besides," Joss cut in, "why should only humans hold powerful weapons?"

"But why your opposition to Rakgar?" Milah growled. "What did he do? He's no enemy."

"That can never be certain," Rylan explained while replacing the sword on his back. "You may be correct; perhaps he only disagreed with the proceedings here. He might have been merely disloyal to a person or thought or idea here, but I don't believe it stopped there. I've never seen such a powerful reaction to the sword."

"Then what about me?" Milah said. "I'm loyal to Rakgar. Does that make me a traitor? Are you going to ask me to leave?"

"That depends," Joss answered.

"On what?"

"Do you believe that the dragons and centaurs should fight the humans?" Joss asked. "Together?"

Milah ground his teeth. He looked to Mitashio, who dipped his nose slightly at his brother. Then his eyes found Hiro, but they came to rest on Prak. Milah narrowed his focus on the little brown dragon. Prak sat up a little straighter.

"Yes," he finally answered. "Yes, I believe we should defend ourselves from the human threat."

"And that," Rylan said, "is why the power of the sword hasn't forced you away."

"That's why we're here," Joss announced for all the centaurs and dragons to hear. "We believe the centaurs and the dragons can work together to combat the human threat to the dragons. No one," he said, specifically addressing the dragons behind Hiro, "will force the dragons to fight. We may not be numerous, but the centaurs are willing to die to protect the dragons. If you don't want us to join the fight alongside you, you are welcome to leave, but I urge you to stay to your caves. Keep away from the surface. It is dangerous for you now more than ever."

Hiro and Tog and Prak looked around. Hiro thought Milah and Mitashio would leave in allegiance to Rakgar, but they stayed. Mitashio started to petition Milah, but Milah shook his head at his brother. None of the other dragons left.

"Alright then," Ashel smiled again, "now we have some planning to do."

10

Rivals

"Forty?" Philip couldn't stop his eyes from popping open. "It's only been a week!"

"Contain yourself," Torgon urged from beside him. "Don't let Anna see you, you'll never hear the end of it."

Philip quickly composed himself as he approached the women's training area on the field. He forced a smile as he watched the imposing group.

No one dropped their swords because now they all held much smaller and lighter sabers, easier to handle and wield. They were most likely blunted for practice, but each woman held the same new weapon. He thought at first appearance that they all wore black skirts, but as they lunged forward he could see a separation in their skirts, much more like long breeches. Blue tunics with leather corsets covered their tops, while their forearms sported leather coverings. Altogether, their wardrobe had a unifying effect.

The women swung their swords together in time as Tierni called out the movements. Anna walked by the women with a long stick, lightly tapping them on a shoulder or knee with correction, to adjust an arm here or bend a knee there. Philip distinctly remembered Bragon doing the same thing with him when he trained as a young boy.

However, the most surprising sight was off to the side of the main group. General Tommak sparred with the larger woman Philip remembered from his first visit to the women's training field the week before. The woman almost matched Tommak in size although neither was as tall as Philip. She swung the same broad sword as Tommak's and the men's, although her dress and appearance matched the women's.

As Philip and Torgon approached, Anna nodded to Tierni and went to greet them.

"What a difference a week makes," Philip said.

"Yes," Anna nodded with a smile, "Tierni and I have been working hard. She's extremely talented, Torgon."

"Talent has nothing to do with it," he grunted back. "She's watched and copied everything father and I have worked on while we're in our home. He's never stopped her."

Anna nodded. "I suspected."

"What uniforms do you have them in?" Philip asked.

"Well," Anna said, "Everything has a purpose and a practical use. The blue tunic is for the Noble Kingdom, of course."

"And the corset?" Philip asked. He forced his face not to flush while saying it but he wasn't sure how successful he was. "What is the purpose of wearing your undergarments on the outside of your clothing?"

"Actually," Anna grinned, "it's lightweight armor." Both Philip and Torgon turned to stare at her. "It's true," she said, laughing. "Using a careful process, the leather has been hardened using dragon fire. The burnishing makes the leather lightweight, waterproof, and nigh on impossible to cut through. Much easier for the women to move in and it keeps them safe as well."

Philip shrugged and shook his head dismissively. Until it was proven to him he would have a hard time imagining that leather could prevent a death-stroke from a good broadsword. "And Tommak?" he indicated the general and the woman sparring. "Have you roped him into teaching you as well?"

"Actually," Anna said, watching the two train,"they were talking yesterday and decided to be training partners today. The first I heard of it was when Tommak approached Hilde this morning."

They watched in silence until the swords stilled for a moment of instruction, then Philip called to Tommak. "How goes training, General?"

Tommak smiled and waved a hand at his sparring partner. "These women are amazing!" he called back.

"Are you willing to help train them, then?" Philip asked.

"I would," Tommak said without hesitation, "only I feel as if I'm learning more from her than she is from me!"

His student, Hilde, giggled sheepishly. Torgon's eyes bulged as he turned back to Philip. Anna giggled under her breath.

"Well," Philip said, turning back to Anna, "it seems this endeavor is doing well. I'll leave you to your practice."

"Actually, Philip," she said before he could get too far, "I was hoping we might discuss something for these women to do."

"What do you mean?" he asked, turning back to her.

"I mean, they are working hard, training well, and learning fast," she said. "Now they need a goal to train toward. They need a purpose."

"A purpose?" he said. "You're not suggesting I put them in the army alongside the men, are you?"

"No," she shook her head. "I think it's far too soon for that."

"Too soon?" he started. "You can't possibly think—"

"Protecting you!" Torgon spoke before Philip could finish his thought. When both royals turned to look at him, he said, "Perhaps they should be protecting their princess. You could have your own private security detail that can go wherever you go."

Anna's eyes bounced between the two men, obviously anxious to pursue the first argument, but unable to ignore the practical offer. Finally, she smiled. "I think that's a wonderful idea, General Torgon."

Once she returned to the group, Torgon smacked Philip in the arm. "Don't start arguments you can't finish, man!"

But Philip's mind had already shifted. "Do you think she's building an army?" he said, watching the women swing their swords with deadly accuracy.

"Why would she do that?" Torgon asked, not entirely discounting the possibility.

"I don't know," Philip said shaking his head. "But why would she need women alongside to protect her when she can wield a sword herself?"

"They're coming," Prak whispered as he set down.

Hiro, Ashel, Tog, and several centaurs Ashel referred to as a squad hunkered behind boulders in the hills. They had flown northwest to intercept a small group of humans traveling to the west. Ashel maintained that they were either bringing supplies or messages or both to the Allegiant or Just Kingdoms. Those were the groups Ashel said they should be picking off.

Easily one hundred men drove wagons or walked alongside them through the valley road. Gold tunics glittered in the warm summer sun. When they came into view Ashel nodded to Hiro and she and Vikal trotted off into the trees on the hillside. The entire squad followed them. Hiro would have expected the sound of nearly twenty centaurs trotting through the woods to be like thunder during the fall rains, but their steps were as hushed as snow falling on the mountainside.

Hiro, Prak, and Tog crouched behind the boulders in the summer sun.

"Hiro, are you going to challenge Rakgar?" Tog asked as they waited. Prak turned to glance at them from his post, watching the group of men approaching.

"Why would I do that?" Hiro asked.

Tog shrugged. "You've never really agreed with authority figures, but I've never seen it this bad between the two of you."

"Just because we disagree doesn't mean I want to lead anyone," Hiro said. "Or be named Rakgar."

"You're leading us now," Tog said.

"No," Hiro shook his head, "Ashel is doing the leading."

"I'm following you," Tog said, "not Ashel."

Tog looked at Prak. Prak nodded to him, then to Hiro, then turned away to continue watching.

"I have no desire to lead," Hiro insisted. "I can't say what is going to happen. Perhaps you should ask Ashel."

"That's him," Prak finally said, without looking at the other two.

"Who?" Tog asked.

"The last man," Prak answered. "The one in back, holding the flag. He's the last man in the group. They're all in the canyon now."

Hiro nodded. "Time to go."

The three dragons launched into the air. Hiro knew the centaurs would be watching for them. They flew over the convoy, circling the tops of the wagons. A fleeting thought that Anna might be with the humans shook Hiro's mind for a moment. As it did, his fire guttered. Hiro blew a little fire and got his mind back into the fight.

Once they got within range, the men guarding the wagons started shooting arrows into the sky. Hiro dodged a couple but caught the third one with his claw in midair. Inspecting the tip, he saw no black marks on it.

When he saw that the arrows were clean, Hiro dove straight for the wagons. Using his fire, he torched a couple of them while the men flung themselves out of the way. Tog and Prak did the same. Tog, using the distinct advantage of his toggling eyes, could dodge the arrows and spears thrown at him, all the while burning the wagons to ash. Prak used his nimble skill and speed to attack the men shooting the arrows.

As the men looked to the skies for the three dragons, the centaurs attacked. Most of the arrows caught the men in the neck as they watched the dragons overhead. The centaurs' deadly arrows quickly dropped a good portion of the outer group of men. The remaining humans tried to gather around the wagons, but concentrating their number only made it easier for the centaurs to shoot them down en masse.

Once the centaurs were close enough, Hiro could watch Ashel's deadly talent. The knives around her horse's body were put to good use, although she didn't throw them unless absolutely necessary. The other half of the squad rushed in from the other side of the mountain, flanking the group of humans. It ended in a matter of minutes.

As the centaurs finished the last of the men, the dragons dug through the burning wagons.

"What's in there?" Ashel asked, standing away from the flames.

"Nothing," Hiro growled. He lifted clumps of burning cloth in his claw for her to see.

"Clothing," she said, wrinkling her nose as if it smelled bad. "No weapons at all?"

As she trotted to the wagon Prak was scouring, he held out dried leaves and fruits. One container began popping rapidly until Ashel told him to roll it out of the fire.

"Cotran," she said. "It's just a food."

Vikal trotted up behind her. "Save that," he said, "we can eat it."

Vikal and the other centaurs helped salvage the food suitable for them to consume. Everything else, the dragons gathered and burned. Including the human bodies.

"It's more than they deserve," Ashel said, while watching.

"We're not monsters, Ashel," Prak said. "If we burn their bodies so they can move on to the World of Souls, we will."

"If they had their way, they wouldn't allow your bodies to burn," she told him.

Prak shrugged off the comment. "That's what makes us better than them."

Hiro stepped beside them. "What do you think?" he asked Ashel. "Was this a success?"

After a moment of thought, she nodded. "Yes," she said, "it was a success in the fact that we are decreasing the enemy's numbers and supplies. But it wasn't a success in the fact that we didn't find any poisoned arrows. I believe we should continue these attacks, even covering the outskirts of the armies that are approaching the Rock Clouds. We can shave their numbers, cut off supplies, and isolate them from their allies."

"But will that be enough?" Hiro asked.

"If all five kingdoms reach the Rock Clouds and succeed in getting aloft into the Rock Clouds, no," Ashel said, staring into the fire. "We don't have the numbers. The dragons and the centaurs will be slaughtered."

11

Opportune Deliverance

"The people of the Courageous Kingdom were and are appalled by the choice our king made in our behalf. King Torodov, as well as all the men, women, and children of accountable age, send you our deepest and most sincere apologies for the decisions made and the actions taken, or rather not taken, to aide our allies of the Noble Kingdom in their hour of need. I have been sent," the servant paused as she knelt in front of Philip, head bowed, then continued, "as a representative of our people. If King Philip or the Noble Kingdom sees fit to end my life in retribution for the heinous lack of courage shown by our people, you shall do as you see fit. Know that my life has been volunteered to either serve you or end for our betrayal, and to restore the honor and courage of our people."

Philip stared down at the sandy blonde hair of the girl in front of him. She could be no older than Philip himself. How could he choose to end her life?

"Tell me," Philip said, "how was your life volunteered?"

The young woman looked into Philip's eyes. Philip didn't see a drop of hesitation. Only resolve. Courage. "I volunteered."

"You volunteered to die?"

"If necessary."

Philip tapped the hilt of his sword. He stood in the receiving hall, a small, quaint room meant for visiting briefly with messengers or visitors to the castle. He had been on his way out when the messenger—The Voice of the Courageous Kingdom, as was her formal title—arrived.

The young woman's steady gaze didn't waver. Philip realized that he could draw his sword and strike the girl down where she knelt, and The Voice would probably still stare into Philip's eyes after the blow struck.

"How did you come to earn the title of The Voice?" Philip asked. He didn't yet know what to do with her.

"I attended a meeting of the leaders and the community," she said, her gaze never leaving his face. "The people decided that King Torodov had made an erroneous decision not to aid the Noble Kingdom when a monster was attacking. I volunteered to bring the message of the people to the king."

"When you volunteered to bring the king the message of the people, did you know that you would also be chosen to bring me this message and be named The Voice?" He wondered what kind of person would volunteer to possibly die.

The young woman seemed perplexed for a moment before answering. "When I volunteered to bring the message to the king is when I was named The Voice," she said. "King Torodov chose not to kill me, but to send me to you to allow you the decision whether I should live or die."

The Voice said it with such conviction that Philip knew the young woman would consider being killed an honor. "Is this often the way in the Courageous Kingdom?" he asked.

The young woman thought for a moment. "Is it not courageous to stand up for what is right? The king and his people respect courage. It is who we are."

"But," Philip had to clarify for himself. He had been taught of the courage of their kingdom, but had never seen it put to such lengths before. "Do the people stand up to your king often? Does he always listen to their word?"

The girl looked at Philip as if the king had sprouted a third eye. "The king listens to courage. Is it not courageous to stand up for what you believe? Is it not courageous to stand up to a friend or leader as much as to an enemy? Is it not courageous of our king to be willing to listen to the opinion of those less noble than him? His is one of the strongest beliefs written in our kingdom: the most courage one can have is to question one's self."

Philip nodded thoughtfully. He knew he couldn't kill the girl. The words she spoke, the conviction she had, rang true to the ideas that Anna had repeated for so long. People could stand up to the king. It was noble and just, courageous and honorable, and indeed loyal in the end to the kingdom to do so. Standing up for one's beliefs had all the qualities of every sword of the Five Kingdoms. People should always have the ability to respectfully speak up and point out their errors to their leaders when they appear to be wrong.

"Please, stand," Philip told The Voice. "What's your name?"

"Avantika," the girl replied, as she rose.

"The apology is accepted. I would not strike down someone as brave and bold as yourself," he said. "I will give you three options. You can return home. Or you can stay and join the messengers of my kingdom; they could learn from your courage and wisdom. Or you can stay and join Princess Anna's growing alliance of women who are learning to use sabers and defend themselves. They call themselves The Black Saber."

"Women?" she asked. "Allowed to train with a sword?"

Philip nodded. "Do women of the Courageous Kingdom fight with swords?"

"No," she said, "the men deem it cowardly to attack a woman or withhold from protecting her from other dangers."

"We find it brave and noble for a woman to protect herself." Philip hoped his reference to "we" sounded convincing, but he was unsure who he was trying to convince, The Voice or himself.

Avantika smiled. "I would be honored to join The Black Saber."

"Wonderful," Philip smiled too, "I think you and my sister have many things in common."

He told a guard to show the girl to the newly appointed office for the group of women Anna was training. After she left, Philip tugged on his riding gloves as he continued his original course into the courtyard.

Before he could go far, he saw Anna approaching from the other direction. He rolled his eyes and shook his head.

"I don't have time for this," Philip huffed as Anna joined him. He marched out into the sunny courtyard and took a deep breath of the warm summer air. He looked around at the green grass, the arched open hallways, the curved parapets. Once he left, how long would it be until he saw this place again?

"So, you're just leaving us behind?" Anna snapped as she watched him.

"That's my job as king," he told her, "to protect the people, and that includes the women."

"Then what have we been training for?" she closed her eyes in frustration.

"To protect you, the princess, and the rest of yourselves."

"I don't want protection. I want to come with you!"

"Out of the question," he said. "I'm going to war, not into town." As she groaned, he turned to face her. "Finish the wedding plans. I'll be back to perform the ceremony."

"You could marry us along the way," she said.

Philip grabbed her by the arms. "Continue training the women. You've got a wonderful program going and I believe it will do a lot of good."

Anna's eyes met his. "And Tierni? You'll leave her behind?"

"Yes," he was proud that he didn't even hesitate, "to keep her safe as well as you."

He stomped out of the courtyard to the front gate of the keep. Torgon was already on his horse. One hundred men stood in the outer courtyard to accompany their king and royal general on their way.

As Philip mounted, Torgon leaned toward him. "As planned, the majority of the army left early this morning. We'll catch up to them easily. This way we can experience the faerie's concoction for speed. I'll make sure supplies are getting through, set up rendezvous points, touch base with the generals, and send the army ahead to the Rock Clouds. We should make it back in plenty of time for the wedding."

"Very well," he raised his hand to the men, who saluted. "Do we travel with any faeries?"

"Not yet," Torgon reported. "Qialla will leave after we do and go straight to meet the army. He's taking a small group with him. We will rendezvous with two faeries while travelling with the main army contingent. Kradik is in the north with Murzod to make sure the poison is finished quickly and dispersed."

Philip pursed his lips. Turning to look at Anna, he waved as she stood with her arms folded across her chest. Before he turned away, her expression softened. "Philip," she called to him. "Be safe."

He nodded and kicked his horse to set it walking. Torgon called to the men and the large party marched out of Kingstor Noble.

12

Surprising Resistance

A pure white wolf lay panting on the soft grass of the forest floor. The container, usually strapped to the beast's belly, lay next to it. Ashel stood over the messenger, reading a parchment, when Hiro, Tog, and Prak stepped up to her.

"Any word?" Hiro asked.

"Not much," she sighed. "It's been weeks, yet no sign of the poison."

"Perhaps we destroyed all of it when I attacked the post with the Ice Ruck."

Ashel rolled the parchment and tapped it against her palm. "Perhaps," she mumbled absentmindedly. "Still," she pulled a large bone with scraps of dried meat on it from a pouch around her waist and threw it to the wolf. He laid into it with a soft growl. "I would have expected something by now. The Gold Army is now camped at the base of the Inner Mountain. We've had reports of seeing the Silver and Black Armies on the move as well. All of the assigned groups are continuing the attacks on the convoys and transports and any other small groups, but some are still getting through. We can't possibly keep up with all of them and eventually we'll have to return to the Inner Mountain to fight."

When Vikal approached, Ashel tossed him the parchment roll. "Anything?" she asked him.

"More of the same," he said, glancing over the contents of the paper. "We've only seen single riders leaving occasionally. Nothing worth attacking."

They had camped near what Ashel insisted must be the distribution point the humans had used for the poisoned arrows for several sun cycles. When Hiro explained attacking a human encampment with the Ice Ruck, how the faerie had tried to kill him, and the barrels of poisoned arrows, she was adamant about these buildings being the human's distribution point. This camp overlooked a small canyon leading through the Torthoth Range west from the humans. Prak led Tog and Hiro accompanying Ashel and Vikal across Avonoa to this position. They all wanted to keep an extra close watch over the facility.

"Perhaps," Prak spoke up, "we should take this time to approach the Ice Ruck."

Hiro glanced to Ashel, who shrugged her shoulder. "I'm sure we can survive a few days until you return."

"Actually," Prak sat back on his haunches, "I thought maybe I should stay here."

Hiro's eyes popped open. He turned to Tog, who shared his shock. Prak? Not want to go see another distant, exotic place as well as meet new dragons?

Hiro shook his head a little, "Prak, I don't see you."

Prak waved away the tongue-in-cheek comment. "I know, I know," he said, "I meant that three of us don't need to visit with the Ice Ruck. The dragons are spread thin as it is. I'm sure I'll meet them when they come to help and I'll probably get the chance to see their home later. More important things are happening here and now. In fact, I don't think Tog needs to go with you, either. If both of us stay here we can continue any attacks with Ashel and Vikal. Since you know the Ice Ruck already, you, Hiro, are really the only one who needs to go."

Hiro looked to Tog, who wagged his head from side to side before answering, "He's got a point. It only requires one to take a message."

Hiro watched the internal struggle on Tog's face. He knew his best friend thought about Visi's words to him. Hiro could see the pain creeping into Tog. "Not to worry, Freeg," he said before Tog could object, "my greatest need for you now is elsewhere, not with me."

Ashel nodded. "It would be best to have the help here in case a large group comes through or we find a lead on the poison."

"Very well," Hiro nodded, "I'll go to the Ice Ruck alone and I'll be back in a few days."

"Hopefully," Tog said, "with help."

Tierni caught another blow from Anna's sword just in time and felt the reverberation through her gloves and down her arms.

"I don't care what my brother thinks he wants," Anna swung her sword toward Tierni's ribs with more force than Tierni thought was called for in the moment. "After my wedding, we're going with him whether he likes it or not."

Tierni's sword shook with the force of blocking the princess's attack. "And if he refuses?"

"He won't," Anna growled as she reset her stance.

They both moved in the same moment. As the maid countered, the royal countered. Their swords swung past each other without touching. Tierni recovered first because she hadn't put as much energy into the swing. Knowing this, she easily countered again when Anna's momentum forced her shoulder to turn too far. The maid rapped the princess on her back.

Tierni allowed her weapon tip to fall to the ground. "I believe that's the first time I've actually taken a match without you allowing it to happen," she said with a small smile.

Anna nodded and matched the grin. "You're much better than I realized," she said, straightening and loosening her armor. "I shouldn't go so easy on you."

"At least you can be assured the group will be in good hands while you're away at war," Tierni said, unstrapping her gauntlets.

The two turned to scan the other women training near them. Nearly forty fighters yelled in time to the commands of Hildegard. They all wore matching uniforms and armor and swung lightweight sabers. A couple partners around the edges sparred with each other. The alliance had grown and looked formidable indeed.

"That's true," Anna said as they watched, "Hildegard is an excellent teacher."

Tierni paused before she mused, "I'm not sure my mother would enjoy the idea of me giving her my papers to go to war. That would leave her and my younger brother here on their own."

"Perhaps," Anna said, taking a deep breath, "we should bring your mother with us. She could help us keep everything organized."

"She might appreciate that," Tierni said, removing her armor.

"Even though it would likely be dangerous?"

Tierni raised an eyebrow at Anna. "I guess I get it from her because neither of us enjoys being left behind."

"Good," Anna said, searching around them again. "You speak to your mother then. We'll need her help to gather the women who will travel, and direct the ones who will stay here with Hildegard."

"But first...?" Tierni stared into Anna's eyes.

Anna sighed and stabbed her sword deep into the grass in front of the sword rack. "But first, a wedding."

"Have you returned your mind?" Rakdar, the female leader of the Ice Ruck, had always looked extreme to Hiro, with the sharp angles of her purple head, but never dangerous...until now. "We're not going to war. Yours or any other! How dare you come here and beg us—"

"I mean no disrespect!" Hiro blurted out before he lost his chance. "On the contrary, I only request your assistance because I know the Ice Ruck is formidable. And logical."

"When you came here before," Rakdar crouched low in an attack stance, "you had proof of a nearby danger. Very real. Very tangible to our ruck."

"This is a very real—"

"—threat to YOUR survival!" Rakdar growled at him. "Had you been part of my ruck I would have struck you down for speaking at the time of the last attack. I let you get away with it because I thought your Rakgar would chastise you. I helped you because the threat was immediate! You have no idea if the humans are even—"

"No idea?" Hiro roared. He'd had enough of this. "Human armies are on our threshold! The centaurs gathering are willing to lay down their lives for our protection! And you can't be bothered to help us?!"

"Centaurs?" Sormano, present but silent since the two dragons started quarreling, finally spoke. "What are the centaurs doing?"

"Helping," Hiro growled at him, but he brought his temper into check before he continued. "They are assisting our attacks on human supply groups. We're hopeful that with the centaurs' help we can keep any poison from getting to their armies."

"Then what do you need from us?" Rakdar grumbled.

"We don't have enough dragons who have passed the Krusible to go with the centaurs," Hiro said, carefully turning back to Rakdar. He didn't want to upset her more, afraid she would see things as Rakgar did and refuse any assistance at all.

"That's too suspicious," she hissed at him. "An animal would never organize with centaurs to attack the humans."

Echoing Rakgar's words, Hiro cringed inwardly. "We leave none alive. The centaurs obscure any trace of dragons from the attack sites, but it's getting more difficult to carry out the goal with fewer dragons to assist."

Rakdar glared at him, but eventually sat up from her attack stance. "I see reason in arguments both for and against helping you."

Hiro waited a moment before asking, "Will you help us?"

Rakdar looked to Sormano, but Sormano didn't move. He might have been a figure carved from the rock itself. Hiro couldn't even tell if he was breathing.

"I see no reason to go," Rakdar finally said, but before Hiro could argue further she continued, "however, I cannot, nor will not, stop any dragon who has passed the Krusible from going."

Hiro sighed with relief. "Thank you, Rakdar," he said, dipping his head to her in respect.

"Might I make a suggestion?" Sormano finally rumbled from the side. Hiro nodded and Sormano stretched his neck out. "Don't send all the dragons with the centaurs. Allow some hunting groups to do what they do best. You'll be forced to eat horse meat, but it won't seem out of the ordinary for dragon behavior."

"A wise suggestion," Hiro said, dipping his head to the older dragon. "I'll bear it in mind."

As he turned to leave, Rakdar called him again. "At least take some flarote with you," she said with cautious hesitation. "We want to see our allies victorious."

Hiro dipped his head again. With genuinely humble gratitude, he slipped with her into the side cavern where mounds of flarote grew all year for these dragons. Piles there had shriveled upon drying. Rakdar scooped several clawfuls into a hollowed, crystalline rock. The rock itself was lighter than it should have been, so Hiro walked out of the cavern laden with enough flarote to kill half a ruck.

As he gave his thanks to Rakdar and bowed from the cave, he turned to see Maggoran and a few other dragons following him. "We're coming with you," Maggoran announced to Hiro's bewildered look. He relieved Hiro's grip on the crystalline rock holding the flarote. "We've all passed the Krusible and we believe in providing assistance to our allies when they ask for it."

Hiro allowed Maggoran to carry the flarote and the small group took to the skies. Hiro twisted his neck around to look back before leaving the magnificent home of the Ice Ruck. Waterfalls flowed freely and green grass shimmered on the steep slopes of the mountains. The only white he could see was atop the highest mountains at the tallest points. The rest of the land had absorbed the same warmth the rest of the surface world shared in the summer. Hiro wondered briefly if he would ever get to see this place again, or ever be able to explore its many wonders.

Anna would love to visit, he thought to himself. Once he thought of her, his fire guttered again, but he hid the thought away and the sensation passed.

"Don't worry," Maggoran said from his flank, watching Hiro's backward gaze, "they will surprise you. In your time of greatest need, they will be there."

Hiro grinned. "Are you a seer?"

"Close enough," Maggoran grinned back. "I know my sires well."

When the small group of fighters had flown partway through the Torthoth Range, Hiro motioned for them to land. All six dragons set down in a clearing well south of the distribution facility. After settling and listening for danger, Hiro faced Maggoran. Maggoran moved to place his nose in front of Hiro's, but Hiro pulled away.

"We don't have the luxury," he whispered. The Ice Ruck dragons' eyes popped open. One's jaw dropped. Hiro held up a claw to forestall the accusations. "Things are different now," he told them amidst growling, "we must speak with the centaurs and we must speak to each other. The dragons helping us are those who believe the secret won't be necessary much longer. This war is changing everything, among humans *and* dragons."

Maggoran stepped forward. With an uneasy glance toward his friends, he lowered his head as if hoping he wouldn't be seen. "Things are changing," he whispered, "but it might take us some time to get used to it. What is it you ask of us?"

Hiro nodded his understanding. "Three of you need to help the centaurs south of here," he said, trying to come across like the leader he felt he wasn't. "No dragons are there to help them. I believe the leader of the group is called Larens. You should report to him."

Three dragons stepped forward and one took the memory of where Hiro had last seen the centaurs. The dragons would start there and find them. With no more sound, the three nodded to the others and two slapped tails before they flew off to find the centaurs.

Hiro faced Maggoran and the other dragon. "We need to find Ashel and Vikal. They should be east and south of here."

They nodded to each other and, lifting into the sky, the group rose above the treetops to survey the landscape. As Hiro ascended, he saw smoke drifting up from further south in the mountains. He knew the first group would avoid that spot because of the directions he had just given them.

"Hiro," Maggoran strained not to whisper, "what is it?"

"I'm not sure," Hiro said, watching the smoke flutter into the clouds. He turned to Maggoran. The three dragons flew lazy circles in the sky as Hiro decided what to do. His head nodded back and forth between the dragons and the smoke. Finally, he jerked his head back to Maggoran. "I'm going to see what it is," he said.

"We'll come with you," Maggoran said. He passed the supply of flarote to one of the others. "Fly this straight ahead to the others. We'll be right behind you."

Hiro nodded as the dragon left with the flarote, but he warned Maggoran, "Remember to use large circles. No formations. Don't attack. We're only checking it out."

"What if they attack us?" the third dragon asked.

"Get out," Hiro said pointedly. He had already passed all of them the memory of where Ashel and Vikal and the others were camped. "And don't wait for any one of us."

"Dragons!" a short burst tore through the group of men. Philip and Torgon set aside their papers to run to the tent entrance. Torgon threw out his arm to catch the king before Philip could exit.

"Stay here," he demanded. Before Philip could refute, Torgon ducked outside the tent.

Philip stayed at the opening, watching the activity outside. The sun setting in the distance made the tops of the trees look like they were on fire. Men shuffled around their posts and eating stations and stared into the sky. Large fires in the center of the camp burned with two large cooking pots propped over them. Even the cooks held their spoons like swords. Some guards donned their weapons. Others had already attached their swords to their sides or backs. Philip glanced back at his bow and quiver in the corner of the tent next to his pallet. Of course, his sword hung at his side.

Shifting his eyes again to the scene outside, he caught a glimpse of wings and a tail above the trees. He stepped outside the tent to see more, but it was gone. Moments later, Torgon approached.

"No alarm," he said stomping up to the king. "And I thought I told you to stay put," he grumbled as the men ducked back into the tent together.

"I thought I was the king," Philip snapped back.

"Yes," Torgon crossed his arms over his broad chest, "and how would it look for the king to be out there fighting dragons and not allowing his men to do their jobs?"

"Brave?"

"Stupid."

"I can hardly be seen cowering, now can I?" Philip crossed his arms too.

"I'll lead the fight," Torgon said as he resumed his seat on the folding chair next to the king's makeshift desk. "You should direct from afar."

"We both know that's not what will happen when the time comes," Philip sat down as well.

"It doesn't matter for now," the royal general said, turning back to the papers. "It looks as if these dragons were just passing by, but I'll need to send a message about them back to Kingstor. I also directed extra Watch." He paused, clasping his hands together. "Things are getting dangerous. Quickly."

Philip nodded. "I know what you mean. The dragons have never acted like this before. More sightings are reported every day."

"And we're not heading away from them either."

The two men nodded in understanding to each other. "We're asking for trouble," Torgon said. "Are we certain the faeries—"

His words were cut off by another call.

"DRAGONS!"

13

Inversion

Hiro circled over the fires below long enough to see the cooking pots above them.

Humans, he thought wearily to himself.

But what are they doing here? Where are they going? Is Anna with them? They were close enough to Kingstor that it might be possible.

The brief thought made Hiro's fire splutter. He tipped in the air but righted himself quickly. Unfortunately, that's when the arrows flew. Dozens at a time. Zipping into the air around the black dragon, forcing him to tumble out of the way. He thought about trying to catch one to check for poison on it but he didn't have time as he was assailed from below. He roared a warning to the others to turn them away and he heard a couple echoing roars in response. When he twisted his head to watch the others change course, that's when the long staff hit him.

Roaring at the sting in his hind leg, Hiro snaked his neck again. Metal teeth on top of the pole jutted through the meaty upper part of his leg. His leg twitched uncontrollably as icy cold pain ripped apart his muscle. Hiro pounded his wings as he tried to stay aloft, but more arrows tore through his wing membranes. That's when the dragon-killer bolts launched.

As he fought through the air toward the other two dragons, Hiro could hear the bolts shattering tree boughs. One struck firmly through his tail, another carved into his softer belly. The men below shouted as each found its mark.

Hiro decided he might be better covered if he slipped into the trees. Perhaps he could get away on foot. Maggoran roared and blew his fire as Hiro disappeared between the branches below. As Hiro tumbled through the branches of a towering pine, he felt an icy slice of pain on his front shoulder.

The black-tipped arrow thrust into the tree trunk in front of Hiro's face just over the slice in his shoulder. Hiro's vision blurred as he stared at the arrow then moved his eyes to inspect his shoulder. The edges of the slice the arrow had ripped were gray with ash. He could see the red muscle underneath.

I'm going to die. I will never see Anna again, Hiro thought to himself. *It's only a matter of time. How quickly will it happen?*

As the thought came, Hiro tried to push it away, but his fire guttered and shook in his belly.

I'm dying, he thought. *Anna!*

Behind him, the men from the camp cheered loud enough to wake the World of Souls. He heard them calling and yelling as they began to work their way through the forest to the dragon.

Not knowing if he was thinking clearly, Hiro reached down and ripped out the bolts and the pike. He bellowed a roar and belched flame as he pulled them free of the muscle. His blood turned to ash as it fell to the ground in massive globs. The pike tore with it a large chunk of hide and scales. Seeing his own ash sprinkle the ground confirmed his sentence of death.

As his mind cleared, Hiro checked for humans around him. He could hear them working their way through the brush. Grateful for the foliage to cover him, Hiro heaved himself off the forest floor and staggered further into the trees, away from the humans.

As he clawed his way across the dirt, Maggoran ran up to him. Without a word he stopped behind a clump of fallen trees to wave Hiro toward him, pointing at some flarote in his hand.

"Where did it fall?" They heard the humans moving toward them.

Hiro inspected the cut on his shoulder. The poison was made with flarote and more would likely make it worse.

"Is it over there?" The humans hunted among the trees. Swords banged against tree branches, clearing their path.

"I thought I saw it go that way!" The humans could be heard making their way toward the pair, yelling the entire way.

Hiro pushed himself up to standing. As he spread his wings, the holes already present in his fragile wing membranes grew as they tore against the tree branches. Hiro tucked his wings and tried to crawl again, but his leg convulsed and dragged him back to the ground.

"By Tartaku, it's a dragon!" a man yelled. "It couldn't have gone far!" Torches and glowing rocks appeared to swim through the trees surrounding the dragons.

Hiro couldn't move. He waved to Maggoran. *Go!* he mouthed. Frantically, he swiped his claw in the air to urge Maggoran's leave. Maggoran trembled, wide-eyed, jaw agape, but he inched backward.

Go! he mouthed again, but this time, feeling his fire shudder, he roared and belched flame. Gathering what strength he retained, he used his two functioning limbs to claw his way across the ground away from Maggoran.

He heard the human hunters' energy renewed behind him.

"Over there!" many voices yelled at once.

Hiro crawled toward a large copse of green bushes. He had seen its type before. He had sheltered in the same prickly branches outside of Jarek's village while he watched Anna ride away. But these were different. The green leaves had returned to the branches and blood-red blooms burst from the tops and sides.

The bushes were easily large enough to cover him, so Hiro dragged his mangled leg and tail behind the cluster.

What's the point, he thought as he came to a rest. *I'm dying. I'll never see Anna again.*

The cold in his belly shook his limbs in turn, shaking his hiding place.

"Over there," someone yelled nearby, "behind the lyndel trees."

Hiro could feel it. The cold creeping from his belly to his shoulder to his limbs.

Anna, he thought, closing his eyes, *I just wish I could see Anna again.*

He could hear the men through the brush he hid behind. They had slowed their pace but approached him steadily. Cautiously.

On second thought, he thought ruefully to himself, *she would never let me live it down that I was taken so easily.*

The cold rippled out from his belly, sending waves through his legs. He could hear every step the humans took. Time slowed. He curled into a ball, laying his face on the cool dirt beneath him.

Let them find me, he thought, *they'll find naught but ash. Just as long as Maggoran gets away and I can haunt Anna for eternity.*

With one final, bone-rattling shudder, the cold overtook him.

Torgon held his sword in front of him, pointing the tip at the copse of lyndel trees. His heart pounded in his chest. He silently prayed the dragon couldn't hear it.

Why is it always this dragon? he murmured in his head.

He stared into the copse, willing his eyes to see between the dark branches and flowers. One of his men stepped up beside him but Torgon swung his arm out in a signal for the man to stay back. He never felt the need to allow other men to go before him. He didn't want anyone else to get hurt just because their royal general took a step back.

Torgon remembered that only a short time ago, the tide had turned with this same dragon. He and a few men had hidden behind a crop of boulders, waiting to make their last stand against the black dragon, when the dragon had suddenly turned and retreated. He knew it then and he knew it now, there was definitely something wrong with this dragon.

Placing the tip of his sword against the thorny branches of the lyndel tree, Torgon pressed it away. Using a gloved hand, he pulled aside the thick branches at the base, where there were fewer thorns. Thorns and branches caught on his gloves and clothes as he forced his way through the copse of fragrant flowers, but he pressed harder into the plants as his men circled around the edges and closed in from behind him. Parting the last thin layer of branches, Torgon stared down at the shaking creature behind it.

"Is it there, sir?" one of the men behind him asked quietly. "Is it the dragon?"

The men continued their press into the brambles behind him. Other men stood to the side with burning torches stolen from the cookfires. Torgon lifted a fist to halt the men.

Releasing a heavy breath, he let his hand drop. "It's a man."

14

Tragic Memory

Maggoran crashed onto the ground in a heap. Tog knew him from Hiro's memories. Hiro had shown him everyone he knew from the Ice Ruck and everything he had experienced. Tog didn't recognize one dragon with him, but he recognized this younger grey dragon with the usually ready laugh.

"Maggoran?" Tog called to him as he and the centaurs galloped to join the dragon on a rocky ledge. This was the designated meeting area he had set up with Hiro.

Maggoran turned his head to face Tog, but his neck didn't rise. "Are you Tog?" he said in a small voice.

"Yes," he answered. "Is everything alright?"

Prak ran up behind Tog before Maggoran could answer. "What's going on? Are you alright? Were you attacked? Where've you been? Where is Hiro?"

Maggoran flinched, his eyes still on the ground. Silence hung thick in the air.

"Maggoran," Tog stepped forward, "what happened?"

Maggoran's head turned. He shook it back and forth slowly until Tog stepped forward to place his nose in front of Maggoran's.

Immediately Tog's vision was superimposed by Maggoran's memory.

He saw smoke whispering from the tops of the trees. Hiro saying he was going to investigate. He watched from a distance as Hiro was assaulted with bolts and arrows. He watched the long pike skewer his hind leg. He watched as Hiro tumbled into the trees with a wail. Tog heard Maggoran's answering bellow.

The vision shifted to Maggoran tearing through the trees on the ground. He heard the humans shouting. He heard a dragon cry out in pain. Hiro was still ahead. The torches drew closer.

Tog's view stopped behind a large copse, hiding him from the humans. He saw Maggoran's claw beckoning Hiro to follow him.

Hiro lay on the ground. His leg was torn open and great gushes of ash fell to the dirt as he tried to stand. He opened his wings and the holes ripped wider. Hiro's face contorted as he tried to remain silent through the pain.

Go!, Hiro mouthed. Tog knew his friend well enough to know he wouldn't want the humans to find both of them.

Maggoran trembled. Tog's respect for the other grey dragon spiked as he could feel the urgency to flee with Hiro.

Go!, Hiro mouthed again. Then he roared, probably from the pain. He loosed fire for good measure. He was obviously trying to draw the humans away. He was sacrificing himself to allow the other dragon to flee.

Tog heard the human's voices grow louder. He could hear their speech, but he only focused on the black dragon crawling away into a dark, cold bed of thorny bushes. Tog watched as Maggoran searched the trees before he slipped through them.

Tog blinked. Tears stung his eyes, but none filled them long enough to give him visions.

"What is it?" Ashel said behind him.

Tog turned slowly to face the centaurs as Maggoran hung his head in silence.

"Hiro's dead," he whispered.

Prak ground his teeth. "That's not possible." He slunk in front of Maggoran. "Show me," he demanded.

"Tog," Ashel barked. He finally looked up to see her moist eyes glistening and her chin trembling. "I can't receive memories the way you can. What happened?"

"He was defeated," Tog whimpered. "He was shot down by humans and he sacrificed himself so the others could escape."

"Of course he would, you stupid dragon!" Ashel yelled at the sky. "I hope you hear how stupid you are!" she shouted, but her voice cracked on the last word.

"No," Prak snapped his tail, "it's not possible. He's The One. Visi said it herself. She said he was the one—to—to unite—"

"The witch was wrong," Tog snapped.

"She's never wrong," Prak uttered.

Tog stomped his foot. "Then she lied!" he yelled. But he knew she hadn't lied. After all, she had been right about Tog abandoning Hiro in his greatest time of need.

"Lies or not," Ashel sniffed, "it doesn't change what's happening now."

Tog couldn't answer. What did it matter anymore if the dragons were destroyed? If Surneen hadn't been waiting for him, Tog might have flown into the human camp right now and dared them to destroy him as well. He blinked hard, unable to clear the image of Hiro tumbling into the trees.

"You're right," Prak spoke, but Tog only heard the distant voice of the little dragon far away. "We need to continue with our plans."

"Tog," Ashel said gently, "are you still with us?"

Tog couldn't think. What was she asking? What did she want him to do? Didn't she understand? His best friend was dead. The world around him should be dying too. He turned and slowly walked away from her, not knowing where he was going.

"Tog," Ashel called, but he heard Prak answer her.

"Let him go," Prak said. "We can manage without him until he's ready."

"But Hiro," she whispered, "I said the only dragon the centaurs will follow is Hiro."

Prak sighed. "Hiro is gone. Tog is unable. The only question is this, are the centaurs willing to follow me in their stead?"

15

Insanity

The human's words echoed in Hiro's head. "It's a man." What was he talking about? Hiro knew the humans surrounded him. He knew they should be looking at a pile of dragon ash. He felt cold air over his entire body. The cold must have consumed him by now. Was the human even looking at him? Had they gone a different way, were they looking at something else?

Cautiously, Hiro blinked his eyes open. He still had eyes. Or, at least, his soul had eyes. Was he always going to be this cold in the World of Souls? He thought that in the World of Souls he shouldn't be in this much pain anymore either. He turned to inspect the face of the human hovering over him with a sword in his hand, but it wasn't pointed at him. The human's brow compressed as he glared at Hiro. Over his head in the darkening night sky, Hiro saw the shape of a dragon whisper through the trees into the air.

"Who are you? Where is the dragon?" the human barked at him.

Two more humans joined the first on either side of him.

"What is he doing here?" one asked.

Hiro knew the three were looking down at him but he had no idea why they were demanding answers of him.

The third man glanced around. "General Torgon," he addressed the first human, the one with the black hair, "perhaps this man is a victim of the dragon. The beast might still be somewhere nearby."

General Torgon nodded. "Good thinking," he said. Then he shouted to the rest of the group, "Spread out, form a search pattern! It couldn't have gone far. You," he grabbed the third man by the arm, "take care of this man." He pointed at Hiro then scrambled back out of the copse of thorny branches, shouting orders to the other men around him.

The third man, a tall man with stubbly light hair on his head, nodded down at Hiro. "Who are you? You have a name?"

Hiro searched the copse as most of the humans dispersed.

Where are they going? he thought. *Did they realize more dragons were with me? Are they looking for the others?*

"I'm talking to you," the man standing over him said with increasing volume. "Do you understand me? My name is Fredrick. What's your name? Who are you? Where did you come from?"

Hiro stopped searching through the forest and stared into the eyes of the human standing over him. Fredrick.

He's obviously talking to me, but I can't answer him, Hiro thought to himself. *But why would he talk to me as if a dragon could speak? No, not a dragon.*

The pain from the poisoned arrow slicing into his shoulder had been replaced with a cold over his entire body. When he tried to move his wounded leg to tuck it under himself better he felt the gentle touch of human fingers on it.

He jerked his head to see who touched him, only to see his own fingers placed on his leg. Fingers! His eyes widened as he turned to look back at the human. Fredrick wrinkled his brow in return.

Hiro looked down at his hands. Hands! Not claws! He flexed the hand. Open. Shut. Open. Shut. The smallest finger on his left hand ended in a little stump, much shorter than the other hand. Yes, that was his. He was dirty. Blood trickled down his leg from the gash in his thigh. His back felt like someone had stabbed it with a thousand swords. And he thought of his wings. He swung his head from side to side trying to look down over his back, but he couldn't reach his neck around to see it. His hands searched his throat. It was so short!

"What's wrong with you?" Fredrick said as he watched Hiro searching his face for a snout.

He poked himself in the eye and it began to well up with water.

What's happening? He searched his body and mind. *I should be dead and burned to ash. Maybe I am dead and this is the World of Souls.*

Hiro turned and watched as a hairy arm reached out from his body to the other man, Fredrick. Fredrick reached a hand down to Hiro. As soon as their hands touched, Hiro recoiled the strange limb. He wasn't dead; he was human.

"What's the matter with you?" Fredrick yelled.

Hiro struggled and tried to pull his four legs under him, but they felt lopsided. The front two were too short and the back two were too long. He wobbled on the limbs before the pain in his leg and stomach forced him to buckle. He floundered on the ground, grabbing at the pain in his stomach while trying to push away his own body.

"He's naked," a bald man said, as he and another man joined Fredrick to investigate the situation. "What's going on?"

"We're not sure," Fredrick said. "Seems we found a crazy man here instead of a dragon." He indicated Hiro, who was putting his fingers into his miniature mouth and nose, trying to figure out where his huge features had gone. "Fetch him a blanket or something," he told the bald man.

My tail! Hiro remembered the missing limb and pain contorted his face as he tried to spin around to look for it. But pain radiated from his middle, not his tail.

Although he knew his tail had been injured, Hiro felt no pain from where it would have been.

"He's hurt," the third man said, as large as the bald man in the shoulder and chest, but soft-spoken. Even kindly. Hiro could see thin, light brown hair on his head and light colored eyes.

Hiro doubled over with a silent scream as the pain in his stomach tore through his middle. Maybe he would die yet.

"Has he spoken?" the man asked, squatting in front of Hiro. He touched him gently on the shoulder.

"Nothing yet," Fredrick answered. "I've asked him several times who he is, but he just repeatedly turns to look behind him."

Hiro reached up and touched his head. Nothing he recognized. No scales, only smooth fur. He tried to pull it down to look at it, but it hurt when tugged at it.

"I think I know what's going on," the man announced when the bald man returned with a blanket. He tried to stretch it over Hiro, but Hiro pushed it away. As he kicked at the man, pain stabbed through his leg. He reached for the wound, but jumped again when he saw human hands.

"Leave it be, crazy man," he snapped as Hiro blocked his attempts to cover him. "I'm trying to help."

"Yax," the man in front of Hiro said, "let me." He took the blanket and held it low to the ground in both hands. He looked up at Hiro, moving slowly. He pulled the blanket over himself, then pulled it off and motioned to pull it over Hiro.

Hiro, unsure how much he should indicate he understood, watched him. Eventually he allowed the man to gently pull the blanket over his human legs.

Warmth spread gradually into his legs, as if a small fire burned under the blanket. Hiro, confused, looked underneath the cover. As he lifted it, the uncomfortable cool air rushed in. He quickly snapped the blanket down and pulled it over more of his legs.

The third man stood up next to Fredrick and Yax. "My wife is a healer," he explained. "She particularly researches dragon attack victims. From what I can tell, this man has all the symptoms."

"What are those?" Fredrick asked.

"Not speaking is the biggest one," the man said. He squatted in front of Hiro and inspected his eyes. Hiro watched him carefully. "They are often confused. Reclusive. It can be difficult to integrate them back into society. If they do speak again, they sometimes don't make sense and they speak of...strange things. Impossible things. They're often terrified of the slightest things, leaves, rocks, even their own shadow. Or..." he pointed at Hiro as he pinched the skin of his arm. Hiro jerked in pain.

"It's ok," he said to Hiro. He spoke slowly and calmly. He didn't yell at him like the others. "You're safe now. You're going to be alright. We're going to help you."

Hiro stopped struggling. He realized that these men were being kind to him. They were trying to help him, which didn't fit the barbaric treatment he would have expected from humans. Especially from soldiers.

"See," he said, "he needs to be treated gently. Calmly. My wife is very good at it."

"Then I'll put him in your charge, Adair," Fredrick said. "Get him some clothes and see to those wounds. I'll inform the general."

Adair nodded and Fredrick left the little copse. "Come on," Adair waved Yax over. "Help me get him back to camp."

Hiro, resigning himself to accepting their help, allowed them to approach him.

"We're going to help you stand," Adair said. He slid his hand under one of Hiro's arms. When Hiro felt the man's hand contact his back, he cried out. He had meant it as a roar, but it came out sounding strange, and feeling strangled.

Yax disappeared behind Hiro. "His back," he said after a moment of inspection, "it looks as if someone's taken a blade to it. Repeatedly. But the other marks...they're permanent..."

Adair joined him behind Hiro. Hiro knew he couldn't turn to see his back, so he only twisted slightly, hoping to keep the men in his view, but even that didn't work.

"What are those? Faerie tattoos?" Adair whispered.

"Looks like it," Yax said.

"But dragon wings?" Adair whispered again. "And covering his entire back? Sorry," he said, leaning forward so Hiro could see him. "I forget I'm not supposed to use that word."

"What word?" Yax asked, also reappearing.

"The 'D' word," Adair said.

Yax's brows furrowed. "You mean 'dragon'?" he said.

Adair threw his hands in the air. "Don't just say it!" he exclaimed. "My wife said it can send the victim into fits!"

The men stared at Hiro. Hiro stared back at them. Did they expect him to do something? He watched them uneasily.

"Well," Yax said, "it doesn't seem to affect him."

"Come on," Adair said again. "Let's get him to camp."

They laced their arms under Hiro's, making sure not to touch his back, and lifted him gently from the ground. They helped Hiro steady his good leg underneath him.

"You're enormous!" Adair said, as he gazed up into Hiro's face. "I wouldn't be surprised if you're an amazing fighter."

"He's got a tail!" Yax yelled, staring wide-eyed down at Hiro's leg. "Or, at least, the markings of one."

Hiro almost fell over in his attempt to follow the eye line of Yax. He looked down at his leg, the one he'd been laying on top of on the ground. Sure enough, the black outline of his dragon tail was clearly traced down the side of his upper leg. The black lines shimmered as if his scales had been crushed to a fine glistening powder and pressed into his skin. It wasn't nearly as long or tangible as the one he knew he'd had before this, but it was definitely his very own tail.

Hiro's lip twitched in a half-smirk.

"He understood you," Adair said, watching Hiro's face. Hiro looked into the man's eyes.

Should I speak to this man? Hiro thought. *I am now apparently human, after all. Perhaps the rules of dragons no longer apply to me.*

"Come along," Adair said. He lifted the blanket off the ground, wrapping it around Hiro's waist while Yax supported his weight. "He needs a healer and a hot meal."

With one human supporting his weight on either side and the rest of the humans searching the forest for him, Hiro allowed himself to be guided toward the humans' camp.

16

Semblance

"I'm—trying—to—help!" Yax shouted while attempting to pull a tunic over Hiro's head and face.

Hiro, waving his arms frantically, tried to keep the strange clothing from touching him. When Yax finally threw the clothing to the floor of the tent, Hiro roared at him.

I should probably stop trying to roar, he thought to himself. *It doesn't sound nearly as terrifying coming from a human.*

"What's going on?" Adair yelled upon entering the tent. Taking stock of the situation he turned accusatory eyes on Yax, who stood over a brooding Hiro.

Yax pointed to the tunic on the floor. "I was trying to help him dress like you told me, but he won't let me."

"Patience, Yaxley," Adair said. He stepped over the clothing and set a bowl full of a steaming mush next to the pallet where Hiro sat. "Everything will be foreign to him right now. He's confused. Things will come back to him over time, but you mustn't press him."

Adair picked up the clothing from the floor. Turning to Hiro, he held it up next to his shoulders and pointed at it, then he pointed at the one he was wearing. "It's a tunic," he said. He swept one hand up and down his upper half as if to show it off. "You see? We all wear one. Tunic."

Hiro glared at the men.

"See?" Yax gestured toward Hiro. "He's insane. He refuses to even wear clothes."

Adair waved his friend's comment away. Tossing the tunic aside, Adair settled on a small stool next to Hiro. "I brought you some food," he said, lifting the wooden bowl. He put the bowl in his hand and used the metal utensil to lift some of the food from it. Showing it to Hiro, he transferred the bowl to Hiro's cautious hand.

"Don't give him the bowl," Yax complained. "He'll make a mess and we'll have to clean it up."

"We need to let him try," Adair insisted.

"He doesn't even know what clothing is for," Yax said, throwing his arms wide. "How is he going to know how to use a spoon?"

Hearing this, Hiro decided to prove this fragile little human wrong. He carefully took the bowl from him and held it in one hand. It was warm and the steam drifting from the concoction in it made his tongue tingle. He held the bowl steady as he used his fist to lift the spoon. Bringing the spoon to his mouth, Hiro could smell and taste the familiar savor of meat. It mingled with other flavors he didn't recognize, but the result together tasted amazing. As he carefully spooned another mouthful, he tipped a small amount of the contents on his chest.

"You see?" Yax said. "He's going to make a mess."

"No," Adair said using a different cloth to wipe the food from Hiro's skin, "he's trying, and he's doing very well."

As Hiro continued to eat, Adair sat back and watched him. "Now what should we call him? A man needs a name. Even if it's the wrong one for a time."

"Call him Troll for as smart as he is," Yax grumbled under his breath.

Although his hearing wasn't as clear as it had been as a dragon, Hiro noted he still heard the muttered comment from across the tent. He raised his top lip at the man, but stifled his growl.

Seeing Hiro's reaction, Adair glanced back at Yaxley. "What did you say, Yax?"

"Nothing," Yax grumbled, scuffing his foot on the ground.

"No, no," Adair stood and walked over to the other man. "I think he understood you. He reacted. What did you say? I couldn't hear it."

"I said nothing of note." Yax said, unwilling to confess his unkind words. "Maybe we should call him Owyn? It's a common name. Seems everyone is named Owyn these days."

Adair shrugged. "Owyn is fairly common. And simple enough," he said, seating himself on the ground next to Hiro's pallet. "What do you think? Should we call you Owyn?" he asked Hiro.

Behind him, Yax muttered again under his breath so Adair wouldn't hear him. "Simple name for a simple mind."

Hiro couldn't let this treatment continue, despite the danger that had been drilled into him, the trials and training and sacrifices he'd made to stay quiet and get him this far. He realized he needed to use his voice to speak to humans now. After all, he was one. But he couldn't tell them his dragon name; Priya had given him that name for a specific reason in a specific circumstance. That name he would keep. He would need to accept the human name these men were giving him.

He stopped spooning the food into his mouth. Staring at the ground, he swallowed his last bite. "Owyn," he said. His voice was deep and sounded the same as it had as a dragon. But it caught in his throat, as if the sound knew it shouldn't be heard, before he forced it out again. Stronger this time. "My name is Owyn."

Adair sat up. Yax's eyes popped open as the men exchanged looks. "We must have happened on the right name!" Adair said, inspecting Owyn's face. "Sometimes things that are familiar will help shake the victim from their confusion." Adair narrowed his eyes at him. "Where are you from? How did you get here?"

Owyn shook his head and returned to the bowl of food.

"No, that's too much." Adair sat back again. "I should have known better."

Yax sat down next to Adair on the ground in front of Owyn. "I don't understand," he said, "he can talk. He understands us. Why won't he answer now?"

"It's too much too soon," Adair answered. "I'm sure it will all come back in time. But for now, we can only continue to work with him." He gave his friend a sidelong glare. "And be patient."

Yax stood up again and excused himself for the night, with one last glance and a shake of his head for Owyn.

When Owyn finished the food in the bowl, Adair fetched a couple chunks of bread. "Bread!" he exclaimed, excited to recognize it. He remembered watching Anna eat it and hearing her explain it to him. Finally, here was something he might appreciate about being human. Thinking of Anna made him start to wonder about what it would be like to see her again, being a human himself.

"Yes," Adair said with a grin. He handed over the bread, and Owyn took a hesitant bite. "You're remembering more. Tomorrow we'll work on wearing clothing."

"Why?" Owyn asked.

"We wear clothing for many reasons," Adair said, handing Owyn the tunic. "Clothing keeps us warm in cold weather, dry in the rain, cool in the summer. It protects our skin from the sun and bug bites and scratches. But most importantly, it covers areas that would be impolite to show other people."

Owyn narrowed his eyes. "What areas?"

Adair rubbed the back of his neck and found fascination overhead on the tent ceiling. "Well, uh, certain, er..." he hemmed and cleared his throat, "...body parts." He finally finished.

"Which body parts?" Owyn pressed.

Adair shrugged and huffed, "Well, mostly, um...the one between your legs."

Owyn threw back the blanket covering him to inspect his body, but Adair tossed his head and turned away. Owyn drew the blanket back over his legs and Adair's gaze went back to him.

"But it's just a body," Owyn said, "it looks like everyone else's."

"Yes that's true, but humans find meaning in being modest about certain things."

Adair then gave Owyn a water skin, which he had also seen Anna use. After he had drunk his fill from it, Adair told him to close his eyes and get some sleep. Adair pulled an extra blanket into the tent and made a place to lie down on the opposite side of the tent.

Owyn watched as the man removed his boots and trousers and even the tunic, then crawled under the blankets. Noticing how closely Owyn watched him, the man shrugged and doused the burning candle.

Owyn lay back under the blanket. He wasn't particularly cold, but the blanket was itchy, like thousands of bugs crawling on and scratching against his body. He would try donning the clothes in the dawn. He remembered the man, Yax, who thought Owyn was inferior, even stupid, before he had spoken. Before drifting off to sleep, Owyn determined that on the morrow he would prove to these men he could learn as fast as a human as he did as a dragon. And adapt even faster.

17

Repute

When the dawn broke, Owyn woke to Adair moving about the tent. Adair dressed himself again in the same style of clothing he had worn the day before.

"May I try some of those?" Owyn indicated the pieces as Adair pulled them on.

Adair nodded and pulled out a stack of neatly folded items he had procured for Owyn the previous evening. He added the tunic to the top of the pile.

"Mine wouldn't fit you," Adair said, handing the pile to Owyn, "so I borrowed these from one of the largest men in camp."

Owyn held up the tunic. After searching it for a clue and turning it over in his large hands, he finally glanced at the other man. "I'm afraid I might need your help," he said.

With an encouraging smile Adair helped him into the tunic. "It's no problem, of course," he said as he pulled the tunic over Owyn's head. "Your full memory will return, with time and patience."

Owyn started to pull the blanket from over his legs, but he hesitated. He looked into Adair's face. "I thought you weren't supposed to see this part of me," he questioned.

Adair nodded, "Normally, no," he said, "but if you were injured or unable to help yourself, it would be ok for someone else to see that part. Like when a mother helps her children."

"Would a mother help her child put its clothes on?" Owyn asked. "Why wouldn't they do it themselves?" He thought back to when his father had helped him learn to fly. His father had waited a suitable length of time, then pushed him off a cliff. If Hiro wasn't ready to fly and didn't open his wings, his father would have waited another moon cycle, then pushed him off the cliff again.

"Children need to be taught how to do everything when they are young," Adair explained. "When they are very small, mothers do everything for them. They feed them, clean them, clothe them, and, naturally, protect them."

"Protect them?" Owyn stopped in the middle of pulling back the blanket.

Adair pinched his brow together as he stared up at him. "Of course a mother protects her children! A mother would never let any harm come to her child. In fact," he helped peel the blanket back from Owyn's legs and carefully pulled his feet over the edge of the pallet, "a mother can be extremely dangerous if she feels her child is in danger."

Taking care not to agitate the dressing that had been applied to Owyn's leg wound the night before, Adair pulled the clothing on him. Owyn watched as Adair put his feet (which looked monstrous to Owyn, with toes that looked like worms) into what looked like white wraps, or covers.

As Adair helped with those and other pieces, Owyn asked more questions. What is this for? Why do I need it? When should I remove it?

"I'm sorry to ask so many questions," he finally told the smaller man once all the clothing had been properly adjusted on Owyn's large frame.

"It's to be expected," Adair said, surprising Owyn again with his patience and understanding. "You've been through a tremendous ordeal. Hopefully, we'll say something that jogs your memory about your life and you'll start getting back to your old self. Until then, ask all the questions you need."

Before he could think of anything else to ask, both men heard a growling sound. Owyn's eyes twitched to the doorway of the tent, then he flipped his head back and forth to search around them in the growing light.

"Easy," Adair said, holding up his hands.

They heard the growl again, but as Owyn searched the tent, he felt his stomach twist in time with the noise. He looked down at his midsection, pulling the tunic up to inspect it.

"No, it's okay," Adair grabbed Owyn's hands as he slapped his stomach to try to make it stop. He avoided the cloth bandage on the side of his abdomen. "It's alright, you're just hungry," he told him. This was nothing like his fires guttering, but it came from the same location inside his new body.

Carefully placing one arm under Owyn's and around his back, Adair pulled the larger man onto his good leg. "Come along," he said, helping Owyn toward the entrance. "Let's take a meal."

Stepping outside the tent, with Adair propped under his arm, Owyn took in his surroundings. More tents were gathered in the grey haze of the morning than Owyn had seen flying over them last night, including several in the trees. Which meant their lookouts on the perimeter were further out than the dragons realized.

Adair led Owyn toward a blackened, burnt out campfire in the middle of the camp. Several supplies had been stacked around the fire pit for seating. Adair steered his charge toward them and helped him sit down. A few men wandered about the trees and amidst the camp, some nodding toward Adair and Owyn. One large, dark blue tent with silver trim loomed over the others. A flag from the Noble Kingdom hung from a pole on one side of the entrance and a man holding a staff stood on the other side.

"Why does that tent look different from the others?" Owyn asked, as Adair dug in a saddlebag next to where they sat.

"That," he said after seeing where Owyn motioned, "is the king's tent. We are honored on this assignment to accompany King Philip and Royal General Torgon."

Owyn immediately tried to stand. "May I speak to them?"

"Hold on," Adair pushed the bigger man back to his seat. "No one speaks with the king. Especially not crazy men who wander around naked in the middle of the night." Owyn glared at Adair, but he continued. "I'm sorry, but only the most elite ever get to speak with the king or royal general. You must have connections far above a staff guard whose wife is a healer." He tilted his head. "Or are you telling me you can remember your life before last night?"

Owyn settled into his seat, shaking his head. "What connections are you speaking of? How must I connect in order to speak to the king?" He couldn't imagine how the king got anything done if he never spoke to anyone. Hiro had ready access to Rakgar as a dragon. How did the king know the best assignments to give his people if he didn't speak to them?

"No," Adair said, "I mean you must know people with greater status than I have who know the king or the general. If you know someone wealthy or affluent—"

"Affluent?"

Adair sighed. "Allow me to get us some food and we can discuss class and politics over breakfast."

The chill in the morning air began to warm and Owyn noticed the men around him gathering supplies. Once Adair returned with another bowl of mush, more men had joined them around the extinguished fire, but none of them were still. It seemed an upset hive of activity in the camp.

Owyn dug into the fog-colored mush in the bowl, expecting the same savory flavor he'd enjoyed the previous night, but he quickly spat the gruel back into the bowl.

"This is not the same bowl as last night," he growled at Adair.

Adair sighed. "No," he said, "and most people have much the same reaction to it as you did. I tried to sweeten it for you, but there's not much to be done about it." He swallowed a mouthful and pointed at Owyn's bowl with his spoon. "Still, it's food and it will give you strength."

With a grimace, Owyn made himself take another bite. It indeed had a sickly taste, nothing like the sweet savor of a fresh kill, but he was hungry and forced himself to swallow.

As he ate, Owyn shifted his body on the bag of supplies. Forcing himself to swallow mouthful after mouthful, he squirmed in his seat. The clothing on him pulled in strange places.

"I feel strange," Owyn said, tugging at the pants wrapped around his hind end.

"What's wrong?" Adair asked, standing up. "What feels strange?"

Some of the men turned to watch, concern etched on their faces.

"I'm not sure," Owyn pulled at the breeches. "I feel..."

"What?" Adair asked.

"Are you ok?" another man asked Owyn.

"I think..." Owyn struggled with how to answer, "I..."

"Tell me what you're feeling," Adair said, "and I'll try to help."

"I might..." Owyn looked into Adair's face, suddenly remembering a conversation he'd had with Anna. "I think I need to chinkle."

Adair dropped his face, but not before Owyn could see the start of his smile and hear the raucous laughter around him. The sound brought more curious faces from tents, even a dark-haired youth peeked from the king's tent.

"Chinkle?" A man across the campfire pounded his fist on his knee. "How old are you?"

The temporarily slowed hive of activity began to move again with laughter and comments. Owyn heard comments on princesses and noble ladies and children in cradles. Someone offered him a sopper or a blotter and something he assumed resembled the under-breeches he already wore.

As the laughter quieted, Adair finally lifted his head to face Owyn. He had to clear his throat several times before and as he spoke. "We...er—that is to say…most grown men, don't usually refer to—erm—*that*…as chinkling." He couldn't stop the rest of his grin from spreading across his face.

"Is it wrong?" Owyn asked, scanning the other men.

"Not wrong," Adair patted him on the shoulder, "just…odd. Most men refer to it as 'the need to sop' or 'sopping' or 'being soaked'. But perhaps 'chinkle' is something you remember from your childhood. No matter." He turned Owyn's shoulders gently to guide him into the trees well away from the other tents. He guided Owyn into the forest where they had been last night. In the back of Owyn's mind, he wondered how many disgusting little puddles he had walked through.

As Adair helped Owyn back toward the campfire ring, another man joined them. Owyn recognized Fredrick from last night. In the growing light, Owyn could see orange hair at the sides of Fredrick's head.

"Adair," Fredrick said as the two men limped back into camp, "is this the same crazy man from last night?"

Adair stood straight as he was addressed by Fredrick. "Yes, sir," he answered. "He's already doing a lot better. We took care of his injuries and he's talking again."

"Talking, eh?" Fredrick looked Owyn over. "What's your name, man?"

"Owyn, er...sir," he stammered as Adair helped him sit on a stump. Most of the supply bags had disappeared.

"Owyn, eh?" Fredrick nodded. "Well, Owyn, we're always willing to take in someone who's lost or needs help. We may not be Hamees, but we do what we can. Unfortunately, your injury will slow down our travel time. So we're going to send you with Adair and two other staff guards back to Kingstor so you can be attended to properly."

Unsure how to react to this news, Owyn nodded hesitantly. Fredrick turned, but gave Owyn a sidelong glance before pulling Adair a few steps away. He lowered his voice so as not to be heard, but Owyn could hear everything he said.

"I'm sorry to stick you with this detail and cut your quest short, Adair, but the man needs to be looked after and we need to get whatever answers we can out of him about the dragon." Adair nodded and Fredrick continued. "You'll be compensated for the entire quest. Just make sure you find out anything you can about the dragon attack. Report to my tent before you leave so you can deliver some reports I have to Kingstor when you arrive. You'll report to me again when we return to Kingstor."

Adair confirmed the orders. After Fredrick excused himself, Adair set off to get more food.

Owyn watched him go and pondered the question of class and how long he could get away with not answering questions about his supposed dragon attack. What did all this mean? What must he learn?

What must he do? He knew this change gave him an opportunity to find a way to Anna. Would he have to go through Philip to see her? Would she believe Owyn was really Hiro as a human? How could he ever explain any of this to Anna or anyone else he knew, Tog, Prak, or any of the others? Would he ever see the Rock Clouds again? Would he be stuck as a human for the rest of his life, eventually buried in a mound of dirt, never to see the World of Souls?

18

Assessments

"There it is!" Adair called out, pointing. "There's Kingstor!"

The foursome had travelled a few days out of the mountains. Owyn recognized the same pathway Anna had travelled with Jarek when Hiro first followed her to find Priya. After those first few days, small villages appeared along the route. The closer they came to Kingstor, the closer together the villages and farms grew.

No beast was with them to carry their supplies, so the burden was divided among them. Although Owyn was the largest man, because of his injuries the other three carried the supplies for all of them. Adair found a strong branch in the forest which Owyn used to assist him in walking, but no matter the added support, he was more concerned about how much his feet hurt in the uncomfortable boots he was forced to wear. Owyn missed having wings.

As they travelled, Owyn asked more questions. "What is this?" "What are those?" "When do you do this?" "Why do you use that?"

"How soon will we arrive? Where are we stopping?" Owyn looked to his companions and recognized the looks he received from the two other guards, Kyle and Hallum, reminiscent of the looks he often gave Prak. Or had often given Prak. Either way, he knew his questions were becoming annoying to deal with.

"I'm sorry," he told the men, "I don't mean to ask so many questions."

Kyle and Hallum insisted they didn't mind, but they dropped their pace and fell behind.

"I'm sorry," Owyn said to Adair, who continued walking next to him. "I don't mean to be a burden."

"It's perfectly alright," Adair smiled. When Owyn hung his head, Adair patted him gently on the shoulder. "No, really. I'm fine with your questions. My wife says after...such a traumatic experience...it takes time to get back to your old self. The only way to do it is to almost relearn how to be a human again."

"Your wife sounds like a learned woman," Owyn said to make conversation that didn't demand answers. "I would like to meet her someday."

"Oh, she is learned. Smartest woman I know. And you will meet her," Adair smiled at the thought, "we'll be at my home on the outskirts of Kingstor by sundown tonight. I don't see any reason to go all the way into the city." He glanced at Owyn. "Unless ... do you think you have business there?"

Owyn shook his head. Only if he could get in to see Anna, but from the conversations he'd had with Adair and the other men, he wouldn't, and there wasn't anything else for him in Kingstor.

"Well," Adair patted his shoulder, "you'll probably stay with me and the wife until your memory returns. Don't worry, we have a spare bed. And I sent a message ahead last night, so she knows to expect us."

Life as a human got more comfortable to Owyn as they journeyed toward Kingstor. Adair gave him another set of clothing because, apparently, humans can smell each other's odor on them after wearing them a while.

Owyn could tell his senses were much the same as they had been as a dragon, but somewhat muted. His hearing and smell were better than most humans, but still not what they had been before he had changed.

As for his vision, he could see clearly farther away than the other men, but not nearly as far as he had been able to see as a dragon. During the day he could see the feathers on a bird in a tree more than four dragon lengths away. But at night, he had the same dim vision as the other men. He realized this as they conversed around a fire one night. Owyn mentioned something he'd seen as they traveled that day and the men marveled at how well he could see, but he lamented that his vision was the same as theirs at night.

"That's not much of a surprise," Adair told him after they had tested Owyn's vision that evening. "Lots of people have brilliant vision during the day, but humans do not have night-vision like some animals do." He chuckled, "We're not dragons!"

Owyn watched the castle grow magnificent as they approached Kingstor. Even from quite a distance away, the edifice seemed to loom as tall as the mountains around them. Owyn slowed his pace to watch the banners and flags flapping in the wind. The pointed and curved merlons that had seemed so menacing from inside the courtyard looked blunted, adding to the regal air from the ground.

"It's breathtaking, isn't it?" Adair said with a hint of reverence. He stopped next to Owyn and stared at the castle. "I'm still awed every time I return home." He clapped Owyn on the shoulder and pointed to a small building nestled among the trees off to one side of the road. "Welcome to my home."

The other men bade their farewells, wishing Owyn to swift health, then continued on to where more buildings clustered together. Adair's home sat well back in the trees, but close enough to the others for community access.

Owyn looked around at the cozy little building. Pots of growing plants crowded together at a corner outside the home. The walls and roof seemed sturdy but weathered. The trees around the home grew so dense Owyn couldn't imagine any sunlight ever shining on it.

As they approached the threshold, Owyn asked, "Why is your home so far from the others?"

"Ah, well," Adair rubbed his neck, "my wife, as I said, loves to learn about many things in both the material and the majikal world. It seems dangerous to other people. They prefer her experiments be done away from their homes. Just in case they go wrong, you see. But they also like us to be close enough that she can help people if they need it. She's very careful with what she learns and what she practices and she's very useful to the village. So, this arrangement seems to work out pretty well."

Opening the door, Adair indicated for Owyn to enter first. Owyn expected it to look like Shampy's hut or Rylan's shelter. He expected it to be bigger on the inside than it looked from the outside and stuffed with majikal ingredients and tools. Instead, the interior was stark and simple. It reminded Owyn of the small portion of home he saw in Eoaa, belonging to the woman who stood in front of her child and died for him. Only the essentials, a bed here, a table, a candle. Perhaps if these people were as simple as the woman, maybe they would also be as self-sacrificing as she was. Perhaps humans could be simple and logical, more so than he realized. Not the brutish creatures the dragons were taught to despise.

"Kiyrti," Adair called into the home. "Kiyrti, where are you?"

"I'm here," a woman called as she stepped in through a back entrance. "Just seeing to the garden. I didn't expect you home so—" she stopped short. Her eyes locked with Owyn's. Hers were kind eyes, a soft bluish-green with creases in the corners, presumably from laughter. She was a small, plump woman and reminded Owyn of the women in Jarek's village. Human women all looked so similar with their plain dresses and simple white aprons, Owyn knew he wouldn't have been able to pick her out in a crowd. Except for one big difference, her belly protruded as if she had swallowed an entire lydik whole!

"Kiyrti, this is the man I sent you word about," Adair said as Kiyrti's eyes rolled over Owyn's large form. "I told you I would be bringing him here." Adair dropped his pack on the ground, stepping toward his wife.

When he touched her shoulder, she seemed to blink out of a trance. It reminded Owyn of when he passed a memory to another dragon. Or used to pass a memory.

"Yes," the woman whispered, "yes, I got the message. It's just..." she wrung her hands on her apron. "I guess he's not what I expected."

"What did you expect?" Adair asked her.

Before she could answer, Owyn couldn't hold back his curiosity any longer. "What's wrong with your stomach?" he asked, staring at her bulbous middle. "Did you eat something too large by mistake?"

Adair's eyes widened, but he said nothing. Kiyrti, however, seemed to relax and even grinned. "Ah," she said, "confusion. That makes much more sense." She rubbed one hand over her stomach and the other toward a bed in the corner. "You must be tired," she said. "We can discuss the birds and the bees later. You'll be sleeping there tonight. Why don't you rest while I get you boys something to eat?"

"Thank you," Owyn dipped his head and shuffled to the bed. Sitting down, no longer needing help, he realized the bed was much more comfortable than the pallet in the tent or the rough ground they had slept on the past few days. He laid his walking stick on the ground next to the bed and fell onto his side. His feet ached and as he lay down he realized how much his back hurt as well. How could humans stand such discomfort?

While he lay on the bed, Adair and Kiyrti moved into the kitchen. They kept their voices low, assuming Owyn couldn't hear their whispered conversation, but he heard every word.

"He's no victim of attack," Kiyrti whispered to her husband. "There's too much dragon in him."

"But he has all the signs," Adair whispered back. "He wouldn't speak at first. He was injured, naked, and extremely confused. When I first saw him, he seemed to be afraid of his own body. He asks questions about everything. Food, clothing, people, everything. He can't tell us anything about his background. He's completely forgotten who he is."

"Did he say the dragons spoke to him?"

When Kiyrti asked this, Owyn took a deep breath. Why would she ask about whether the dragons spoke? Anna should be the only human who knew that truth.

"No," Adair admitted. "He hasn't shown that symptom."

Kiyrti sighed. "Ok, you're right. It sounds like he is a man who's had an extremely traumatic experience with dragons. Maybe that one symptom has yet to show itself. Of course, in some cases, the victim doesn't ever admit something that sounds so crazy."

Admit? Owyn thought, *Admit? This woman sounds like she knows dragons can speak!*

Before he could ponder the question further, someone burst through the front door.

"Kiyrti," a man's voice called, from behind the door. "I'm back! Is Adair returned yet?"

When the man shut the door, Owyn could see his features properly from the bed where he rested. The man was broad at the shoulder and had light hair with darker fur on his chin. His eyes were the same smiling, twinkling eyes as Kiyrti's. They lit up when his eyes fell on Owyn.

Before either of them could say anything, Adair came from around the corner. "Koris," he said, with his arms flung wide, "good to see you, brother!"

Koris and Adair clapped each other on the back briefly. "When did you get in?" Koris asked.

"Only moments ago," Adair said. "This is the man I wrote ahead about." Adair swept his hand toward Owyn. "Owyn, this is Kiyrti's brother, Koris. Koris, this is Owyn."

"Owyn, huh?" Koris said. "Seems everyone is named Owyn these days."

Koris's yellow hair dangled past his ears, not nearly as short as Adair's. But the yellow seemed much dirtier than Anna's thick yellow locks. It matched the color of Kiyrti's hair. Kiyrti and Koris both seemed surprisingly younger than Adair, although Owyn had to admit he probably wasn't the best one to judge human ages.

"We're not sure if that's his name," Adair amended. "But it's the one he's chosen for now. Owyn, if you're able, we can sit over in the kitchen and get some good home-cooked food for a change."

Adair stepped ahead of the other two men into the kitchen, a portioned-off area of the little home. On one wall of the room was a huge fireplace with a large pot and other tools for cooking, as Adair described them. A large platform opened over the fire with a door, pokers for the fire, large wooden ladles, what appeared to be a small spade, and many other tools Owyn couldn't put a name to. To one side was a small table where Kiyrti laid vegetables and herbs and a large portion of dried meat. She stood with her back toward the men as she chopped and scraped and busied herself with the fixings.

Owyn and Koris settled together at another small table near the fire in the small kitchen. He could feel the heat and wondered to himself what might happen if he touched the flames. After a moment, Adair pulled up a chair and motioned for his wife to sit next to Owyn. He then took over her food-making tasks and Kiyrti started asking Owyn questions. "Do you remember anything of the night?" "Do you remember your name?" "What do you know of human behavior?" "How have you felt since that night?" "How do you feel now?" "How are your leg and other injuries?" She wanted to learn everything she could about what happened that night, from Owyn's point of view. But Owyn danced carefully around each question, feigning ignorance when she would ask something too probing.

With the lack of forthcoming information from Owyn, Adair began answering her questions and trying to explain the experience. Adair described where they'd found Owyn, what was happening at the time, and what had happened since. Owyn took note of Adair's perspective.

When Kiyrti's questions slowed, Koris filled Adair in on what had been happening in the village during his absence. Owyn listened to Koris's account and interjected an occasional curious question about the human activity. But during most of the conversation, he pondered what Adair had described as the men's point of view in the forest before they found him.

The men thought they were under attack, he finally realized. *They claim they would only strike if they were under threat, but we hadn't threatened anything. I guess flying over and trying to find out who they were and what they were doing was seen as a threat. At least to an army.*

Eventually, Owyn's silence was noticed. Kiyrti rubbed her belly and looked down at it. "Owyn," she said, "you asked about this." Snapped out of his reverie, Owyn nodded. "Well," she continued, "this bulge is a child."

Owyn jumped to his feet. "You ate it!" he yelled. "I knew it! You're violent! Barbaric! Disgusting! How could you? Your own offspring!"

"No!" Kiyrti yelled back.

"Owyn," Koris started, "you don't understand—"

Adair placed his hands on Owyn's shoulders. With a calm expression, he pressed Owyn back into his seat. "We would never do something like that."

"Never!" Kiyrti huffed. "This child is still growing. It won't be born for more than a month."

"So," Owyn watched the others carefully, "this is how humans come into the world?"

"Yes," Kiyrti said, "when they're born, they need parents to care for them until they grow strong enough to care for themselves."

"But why would you bring such a fragile creature into this world needing so much help?" Owyn asked, indicating the round belly.

"Every species reproduces a small version of their self," Kiyrti said with a sigh of patience. "A child who grows and flourishes from their birth is every mother's dream."

"But other species' offspring can protect themselves from birth." Owyn insisted. "Take the scorrand, for instance. A hatchling can kill small animals and feed itself by instinct from when it hatches."

"Humans are not scorrands," Adair said from beside the cook pot, "and we care for and protect our children and families with our lives. Why do you think I'm in the army? It's not because I enjoy fighting. The army provides a means to support and protect my family."

"Yes," Koris said, as if deep in thought. "The army is the only way to go. It's a perfectly viable option to provide for one's offspring, and especially if one has no other way to earn a living." He looked knowingly at Kiyrti, who shook her head, then turned back to Owyn. "What do you think, Owyn?"

"I suppose that's true," he said, honestly.

"Owyn," Adair began, placing a bowl of food in front of him. From the bowl wafted the scent of the mouthwatering substance he had on his first night as a human. "Koris feels he has no other options to be an apprentice or learn a craft. You appear to be somewhat in the same spot as he is in that regard. Can you tell me, do you feel the need to join the army to earn money? Or do you feel inclined to some trade?"

"Trade?" Owyn asked distractedly as he pondered the food in his bowl. It smelled so good his mouth tingled and his stomach began to feel warm. "What do you mean?"

"A trade, or craft," Kiyrti said as she accepted a bowl from her husband. "Something like blacksmithing, farming, healing, or carpentry. Do you feel inclined to any of those trades?"

Owyn felt as if they were probing him for information. He took a hesitant bite of the stew and wished he could pour all of it straight down his throat. Gulping, he asked, "What are those?"

"What are they?" Koris looked suspiciously at Owyn. "You're probably a nobleman."

"Koris," Kiyrti said, "we must be patient with him. Owyn," she turned back to him, "blacksmiths make things out of metal. Farmers plant and grow food in fields, or tend animals before they're killed to eat.

Healers help people recover from injury or sickness. And carpenters make things out of wood. Do any of those occupations, or ways to occupy your time, sound familiar or interesting?"

Owyn thought a moment. "I think I know someone who is a farmer," he said. "But I don't think I would enjoy tending to plants and animals myself." He scooped a large chunk of brown meat from his bowl and stared at it intently. "I much prefer to eat animals."

"Mm-hm. You see," Koris said between bites, "you shouldn't do something you won't enjoy just because you can make money doing it. I'm joining the army and I think I'll enjoy it."

"But the army *is* dangerous," Adair said. "It's for that reason we're paid as well as we are."

"But it hasn't been dangerous until recently," Koris argued. "I'm sure once we take care of the dragon threat it will—"

Kiyrti cut off his words with a gasp. Placing a hand on Koris's arm, they all three looked at Owyn. He remembered what Adair had said about victims of their attacks reacting to the word "dragon". They watched him for a response.

"It's ok," he finally said, "that word doesn't upset me."

"How odd," Kiyrti mumbled. Placing her spoon in her stew, she stepped over to Owyn. He let her put her hand on his forehead before she pried his eyelids open to peer into his eyes. She looked intently into them until her husband bade her to sit.

"Anyway," Koris said, ready to change the subject. "They're bulking up the army for the war. There's an induction in two days. I'll be there."

"Induction?" Owyn asked, also eager for him to change the subject, and he wondered if Anna would be there.

"Yes," Koris explained. "That's when you can sign up to train as a staff guard. They'll house you and feed you and clothe you while you train. And even pay you for it. Then, if you pass the training, you swear fealty to the crown and receive your assignment."

"How about it, Owyn,?" Adair chuckled. "If you want to meet royalty, you can see them at the swearing."

Owyn almost dropped his bowl. "What do you mean?" he asked, sitting up straight at the thought.

Adair glanced at his wife. The look held meaning, which Owyn tried to ignore. "I'm sorry," he said, "I was only joking."

"No," Owyn pressed, "what are you talking about?"

Adair glanced at his wife and her brother, but they said nothing. "You mentioned before," Adair said, turning back to Owyn with a kindly tone, "you wanted to talk to the king or someone that knew him."

"Yes," he answered, "but you told me I didn't have the right status to see the king."

Adair hemmed his answer, but his brother-in-law spoke. "That's just it," Koris said, "everyone gets to see King Philip close up, when they swear fealty to the crown and join the Noble Army."

Perhaps Anna might attend as well.

19

Kindling Familiarity

Two days later, Adair, Koris, and Owyn marched together on the road to Kingstor. Owyn's injuries had healed quickly, surprisingly quickly. Kiyrti claimed they must have looked worse than they actually were, or perhaps Owyn was just a fast healer. However, Owyn began to wonder about the different effects of the dragon poison on humans versus dragons. Either way, he still walked with a slight limp, but retained only scars where his other injuries had been.

Adair explained while they traveled that the meeting with royalty would be brief and no one would have a chance to actually speak with the king. He tried to emphasize that the best Owyn could hope for was an assignment at the castle or within Kingstor. Adair tried to dissuade Owyn from joining the army, but Koris encouraged it.

When Koris wasn't yet an adult he had worked as what the humans called a runner, young men sent with messages between posts and whatnot. He enjoyed it, but he'd just recently turned of age and could join the army, which had always been his goal.

Adair described what he could about being in the army, which wasn't much. Many of the assignments were quite boring. Much of the training was kept quiet, for reasons Adair couldn't or wouldn't say.

"At least we'll each know someone if we both enter," Koris told Owyn. "We won't be in it alone."

Adair separated from the other two men once they reached the front gates leading into Kingstor Noble and the city the castle walls encompassed. He had to part with them to check in with his captain and let him know why he had come back. He hugged Koris farewell and wished Owyn much luck. "I hope your memories return and you learn you are fat with riches!" was actually what he said, but Owyn took the comment only as a well wish. Adair indicated where they should go to join the army and the two men continued down the road.

They turned a corner just past the castle on the side nearest to Teardrop Sea. Next to the castle wall stood a tall, barrier fence made of wood with large wooden gates that stood open, leading to an enclosed area next to the castle with large and small wooden buildings. Several men inside the gates wore the bright blue tunics of the Noble Kingdom. Some men swung long poles in the air; some swung them at each other. None of the men swinging poles wore tunics. Two men in blue tunics stood at the entry, eyeing anyone who came near the gates.

"I don't care what I'm made to do," Koris said, taking in all the men, with or without the tunics.

Owyn couldn't echo Koris's thoughts. He had tried being on The Watch in the Rock Clouds. The Watch was the closest thing to an army for the dragon ruck and he hadn't been suited for it. The only assignment he ever enjoyed was teaching the younger dragons, but he didn't know enough about human life to try that now. Inducting into the army now was his last chance to meet with anyone of royal blood, and Anna. If that didn't work out, he figured after spending time with Adair, Kiyrti, and Koris that being in the army was the only place he could earn money and pay for his own food and clothing. It was his only hope to succeed as a human unless he could figure out how he had changed from a dragon in the first place, and how to fix it and go back. However, if he remained a human for the rest of his life, with or without Anna, he knew he would spend it miserably in the army. Probably fighting dragons.

As the two men stepped up to the gate, the guards in tunics grunted, "Induction?" Koris and Owyn nodded. One guard shoved a thumb toward a man inside, sitting at a table. As Koris walked past him, he heard the guard mutter, "A little short, but we'll take any fresh dragon food. You..." He stepped in front of the larger man, Owyn, blocking his way with a hand on his chest. With a low whistle he shielded his eyes from the sun as he looked up into his eyes. "I wager you'll be a fighter," he said with a grin.

Owyn opened his mouth to question, but Koris grabbed him by the arm. Pulling him toward the table, he muttered, "Don't let them bother you. Adair said guards always give the new men a hard time."

The stench of sweat and filth almost overpowered the noise of the chaos around them, but Owyn pushed it all aside, knowing he would have to get accustomed to it. They stood behind another inductee already talking to the man seated behind the table. After the inductee moved out of their way, Koris and Owyn stepped up to the table.

"What's wrong with your leg, son?" The man behind the table pointed out Owyn's limp.

"It's nothing," Koris said. "He's healing fast."

"Nothing?" the man grumbled. "Some injuries prohibit induction, and that one looks questionable. What happened? How did you get injured?"

Owyn opened his mouth to speak again, not really knowing what would come out. Fortunately, Koris leaned over the table. "It was from a dragon attack, sir."

The man lifted an eyebrow, then allowed his eyes to rake over the tall man. "Dragon attack, eh?" he said, looking all the way up to Owyn's head and making the same motion to shade his eyes as the man at the gates. "I believe the king would be fortunate to have you in his army," he said. "Let me guess, you prefer to be stationed at the castle?" He began writing something on a piece of paper.

"How did you know?" Owyn asked.

The man sighed, "Everyone wishes to serve in the castle. Don't get your hopes up."

The man wanted their names, family names, and where they were from, the last two of which Owyn had neither. But his size persuaded the record-taker to continue with Owyn's induction. Another man measured Owyn for a tunic. Finally, they were told to grab one of the poles and try to get accustomed to it while they waited.

That was the end of the induction process. The new inductees in the yard whiled away the time getting comfortable using the long wooden poles. Several men in tunics walked around the yard, showing them how to hold and swing the weapon, which end to strike with, where to place their feet, etc., but no formal instruction was given to the group. Finally, as the sun went down, a horn blared and the two men standing at the gate began to close the giant wooden structure.

Great, Owyn thought, *I'll probably be closed in here for the rest of my miserable human existence.*

"Men!" came a shout from over their heads. The building on the far side of the enclosure from the gates had two sets of staircases, one on either side, which led to a balcony that ran the length of the structure. A man with dark skin and no hair on his head stood at the balcony railing, looking down on the men in the courtyard. He wore a clean, blue tunic with four small swords decorating the shoulder. His hands rested on the hilt of a silver sword on his hip.

"My name is General Tommak," he said as the men quieted. "I have the honor of serving Kingstor and its province. I am in charge of new inductees and their training. You have been inducted into the greatest army in Avonoa. You will be taught much in the next few weeks. Fighting with a long staff, fighting with your hands and body, and even some swordplay." A few men murmured and jostled each other. "It won't be easy work. You will rise early and retire late. You will be pushed to the edge of your endurance and asked for more. But this is because the Noble Army doesn't accept the weak or faint of heart. Serve your king and your country with all you possess, and your king and country will serve you.

"As many of you know, King Philip has declared war on the dragons." As Tommak continued, Owyn's stomach clenched and burned at these words. "We are accepting more men into the army than ever before because the need will be great in the coming weeks and months. Divisions are already marching toward the dragons' home in order to prepare for the coming war. Time is short.

"Normally, training would last two months or more before a candidate would be tested for their acceptance into the army. But we don't have that luxury of time, and many of you will test within a few short weeks. After that, you will likely receive your marching orders to join the rest of the army on the front lines. Listen to your instructors and learn well. Good luck to all of you, and I hope to fight alongside you at the Rock Clouds."

Owyn's heart burned at the name of his home, the Rock Clouds. Tommak said it. The war would begin in the Rock Clouds. If only he could get this information back to the ruck. But without wings, that would never happen. Maybe since he'd joined the army, he could go with them to the—

"Owyn," Koris pushed him from his side, snapping Owyn's focus back to the present, "come on. He called our names."

Owyn realized another man had taken Tommak's place on the balcony. He was directing the men below him by calling out their names and pointing at them to join one of several groups. Owyn allowed Koris to push him into theirs. A few of the men stared up at Owyn briefly before turning their attention back to another man in a blue tunic standing on the ground in front of them.

"Like the Captain said," the man in the blue tunic said, "my name is Callum. I will be the Lieutenant in charge of your claw."

"Our claw?" Owyn asked out loud. A few of the other men snickered.

"Yes," Callum said, "your claw or squad, as it's properly known on paper, will be Squad 3-4. You ten men will be in the same claw together for your entire training and will probably be given the same assignment, to go to the Rock Clouds when your training is complete. Many guards serve in the same claw with the same men for several years. So take some time now to get to know each other. The closer you are as friends, the easier it will be to trust each other with your lives.

"First things first," Callum continued, "let's get your gear." He pulled out another paper. "As I call your name, step forward and take your bundle. Owyn," he said, then looked up, scanning the men in front of him. His eyes quickly rose to Owyn's. "I see why you needed a specially made tunic. I have one of those for now. You'll get more later. Pick up your bundle and staff." He jerked his head toward a pile off to his side.

When Owyn stepped forward, he took the small bundle of clothes proffered him, then lifted a long wooden staff from a pile next to the bundles.

Koris stepped forward and received a larger bundle of clothing and his staff. Callum continued to call the other names. Maelin was a tall man, a little older than the lieutenant. His staff only came up to his chin. Brandell, a stocky, red-haired youth with a mischievous glint in his eye. Nolan, sand-colored hair and a straight back fit perfectly with the long nose he looked down at everyone from. Taka, a darker-skinned, small young man who looked like he was ready to smile at a joke. Thaddius wasn't as tall as Owyn, but his arms and shoulders bulged with striated muscle. Addil, easily the smallest of the group of men, had suspicious eyes and spectacles perched on his nose. Tua immediately reminded Owyn of the centaurs. He had long black hair, a ready smile, and clapped every man on the back as he introduced himself. And finally, the last name called was Darwick. He was a thickly set man and although he seemed as young as the other men around them, he already had a heavy, black beard, braided down to his chest.

"So, this is it," Callum said. "This will be our claw for training and possibly beyond. I'll show you to your den."

"Den?" Owyn whispered to Koris as the group moved away from the courtyard.

"Yeah," Koris whispered back. "I suppose that's where we'll sleep and live while we're training."

As they loped through the stand of buildings in the shadow of the castle, Callum pointed out other important places. The feed hall, where all the men would eat together at the same time. "Don't be late," he insisted. "If you don't have time to eat, you don't eat. If there's no food left, you don't eat. If you don't want the food that's there, you don't eat."

The training grounds were important to point out as well. "This is where you'll spend most of your time. Rain or snow or shine, you'll spend at least half of every day here." The square of land where he pointed ran the entire length of the castle, all the way to Teardrop Sea. What Owyn could only assume was training equipment lay scattered around the large field. Although he could understand the boulders and ropes and even the extra swords and staffs grouped together, he couldn't imagine why they would use what looked like stuffed pillows.

"Will the officers train here?" one of the men asked before Callum could direct them to leave.

"Officers?" Callum nodded, locking his hands behind his back. "Sure, officers train here all the time.

But if you're hoping to catch sight of the generals and maybe even the king," he gave a half grin, "I'm sorry, but they use separate grounds on the other side of the castle for training. If you're lucky, we might run laps around the castle, but if any of you so much as glance in the direction of the officer and royal training grounds, I'll cut you down myself." He placed one hand on the hilt of his sword to emphasize his words. "Besides, most of the army is mobilizing now. Soon, you'll think you're living in the World of Souls."

The den was part of several smaller buildings huddled together across the training grounds from the castle. They were isolated and easily visible from two of the towers. Owyn thought the army leaders must not have much faith in their inductees if they had to be watched so carefully. He had hoped, being so near the castle, he might find a way to slip in and see Anna. But he could tell the castle guards would likely keep a close watch on their movements. If he wanted to get into the castle unnoticed, he would have to circle around behind the feed hall and other buildings adjacent to the castle. However, he assessed there would probably be more guards there. Groaning to himself, he slipped into the little housing unit for their claw.

The interior was compact. Several structures built of rough wood lined the little room. Worn leather hung between the wooden poles and tethered them. With barely enough space for the number of wooden structures, the men crowded the remainder of the floor. Callum held the door open while the men shuffled inside. Owyn almost hit his head on the top of the entryway.

"These," Callum said when he finally pressed his way inside, "will be your living quarters, or your den."

"There's no mattresses," Nolan pointed out. Owyn wasn't sure what a mattress was, but decided he would find out later.

"There's no bedding," Taka indicated.

"There's nowhere to put our belongings," Tua added in a surprisingly soft voice.

"All things unnecessary to your training," Callum pushed into the room. "However, nobility has its rewards. Once you have proven yourself, you will receive certain items. Your first assignment in here is to decide where everyone will sleep." He walked to the door as the men began to step between the wooden structures. "I'll leave you to it and it will be decided how well you did in the morning. Good luck." He slipped out the door to their silence behind him.

The men spread throughout the room. A few placed their bundles on the leather straps slung between the poles. Owyn stepped to one of the open structures with Koris. The leather straps stretched across the poles from his chest down to his knees. Owyn pressed his hands on the straps at the top, testing their strength. The wooden poles holding them creaked as he pressed.

"I'm not sleeping on that with you above me," Koris said emphatically.

"I don't think any of the bigger guys will be safe on the top," Darwick grumbled.

Brandell, one of the smaller men, chuckled, "Works for me!" He vaulted himself onto the slings at the top of one of the structures. When he landed, the poles creaked and swayed. "See," he said with a smile, "nothing to worry about!" He shifted and turned, but even Owyn could see his back end poking through the bottom, the straps slowly spreading.

Brandell rolled to his side to face most of the men. Sitting up on one elbow, he began to say, "We'll be fine if we—" before his elbow also slipped through the straps and he slapped his face against them. As he made to right himself, his back end slid entirely through the leather.

He yelled as most of the rest of his body also slipped through and got trapped. His middle folded and dangled like an icicle. His arms, legs, and head were held together by the leather bindings. Mistakenly, he clung to the straps with his arms to keep himself from falling all the way through. Koris looked up at Owyn. "I'm not sleeping with your butt in my face," he said.

Taka stepped forward to help Brandell out of his predicament, but he wasn't strong enough by himself. Eventually, Maelin directed Thaddius and Owyn to pull him up by his arms to free him.

Once free of the bindings, Brandell laughed. "Never mind, I'm sleeping on the floor!"

"It's actually quite simple," Addil's nasal voice muttered from behind them. Everyone turned to find him weaving his own clothing from his bundle between the slats of leather.

"How are you doing that?" Maelin asked.

"Will it hold?" Nolan said.

"Probably not someone like me," Thaddius remarked with a glance at Owyn.

The men watched while Addil finished weaving his breeches into the bed. Unfortunately, the only clothes remaining to him were on his back. The rest of his clothing covered two-thirds of the bed.

Addil tentatively pushed his hands on it, adding a little more weight every time. As he pressed, the bed held, but the bottom straps began to separate.

"I have a feeling it will only work if the bed is completely covered," he said, sitting back on the floor.

Owyn realized that the room had grown warm. The little building had only two windows, one in front and one in back, but they were both shut. The hot summer air stifled the little building with so many bodies inside.

Without thinking about it, he pulled off his tunic and tossed it to the little man. "Use this," he said. "I'll probably have more than enough to make my own bed."

Addil grinned and began weaving the finish to his bed.

"Well, that's it then," Taka said, untying his own bundle and turning to another bed, "Addil will be our idea man."

Owyn had to watch Addil a little closer to see how the bed should be done, but eventually he followed everyone else's example. Without his full bundle of issued clothing he actually had to borrow a pair of pants from Nolan, and some of the men had to exchange pieces to finish all the beds. Addil helped figure out who needed what size, but eventually most of the beds neared completion.

As Owyn continued his own bed beneath Koris's, he heard a shout behind him. "What in the name of Fellesi is that?!"

Owyn turned to see Brandell pointing at him, wide-eyed. The others turned to look at Brandell first, then followed his finger to Owyn.

"What?" Nolan asked. "What is it?"

Brandell was pointing at something behind Owyn. Owyn turned to look at his bed, wondering if he had done something wrong. Behind him, he heard gasps and more exclamations.

Someone grabbed Owyn's shoulders from behind and turned him to face away from the others.

"Are those dragon wings?" Owyn heard Thaddius say.

"That's amazing!" Darwick said with awe.

"I've always thought about getting a mark! I've never known someone who could do a mark that's so detailed," Taka said.

"You should see the tail," Koris said, since he had been present when Kiyrti examined Owyn's injuries and markings. After some cajoling, Owyn pulled his breeches down – he needed them to make his bed anyway – to show the tail mark on his leg.

"Is it a special ink for the marks?" Tua asked, noting the way they glistened much the same as dragon scales. For this and most of the questions about his markings, Owyn had no answers.

"Was it painful?" Tua said, finally allowing Owyn to turn and face them. "Was it painful to get such intricate marks?"

Owyn's eyes wandered to the ground. Gritting his teeth, remembering the night he thought he would die made his heart clench. "Extremely," he answered in a small voice.

"Come on, men," Maelin finally tried to shoo the others back to their own spaces. "We're losing daylight."

Koris stepped closer to Owyn. In a low voice so the others couldn't hear, he asked, "Do you remember getting the marks? Are you remembering something?"

Owyn shook his head. "I suppose I just remember the pain."

Koris patted his shoulder. "Well, that's still something."

The rest of the evening passed uneventfully, thanks to Addil's fix for the beds. The men lay in their beds and discussed their lives and reasons for joining the army. Most were there only to earn needed money for themselves or their families. Thaddius wanted to be a fighter, he knew. Maelin had lost his family and wanted to protect others from the same fate. Whenever the questions came around to Owyn, he tried to avoid them, with Koris's help.

"A dragon attack, huh?" Tua said, staring up at the ceiling. "Bet you'd have some stories to tell if you could remember them."

"Is that where you got the scars on your back?" Darwick asked. When Owyn answered in the affirmative, the bearded man sat up to look at him. "Don't worry, we're all going to be together for a long time. We'll help you remember."

Most of the other men concurred. Owyn didn't know what to say. Talk subsided in the gathering dark. Only Taka and Brandell whispered long into the night.

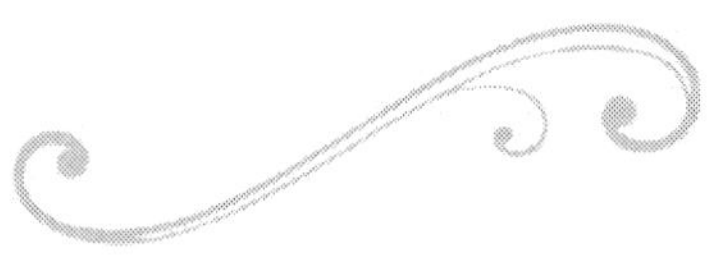

20

Grit

Training for the army was easier than Owyn expected. His muscles were hardened much more so than those of most of the other men, except Thaddius. He could run faster and jump higher and his energy would slow long after the others'. He assumed many of his dragon characteristics were the source of his endurance. Even his senses were keener, leading Owyn to wonder if there was enough dragon in him to somehow fully bring it out again.

Day after day the men trained alongside each other. They ran and lifted rocks repeatedly to gain strength. Owyn felt little progress from most of the practices until Koris explained that the other men must work harder to be as strong as Owyn and Thaddius were in order to complete their training.

Days were filled with hard labor to build strength, practice with the staffs, and a little sword-play. They weren't allowed to use swords, of course, only long sticks. They spent a lot of time running and Owyn eventually got used to the feel of the hard boots enclosing his feet and the chafe of clothing on his skin.

Most of the running and hard labor was accompanied by education. The men learned meanings of army terminology, combat strategy, and even some politics. They were taught practical things like how to clean clothes and cook food. Unfortunately, they didn't have time to practice these things due to the shortened training duration.

Meals were brief and the food never tasted as good as the food Kiyrti had prepared during Owyn's stay with her family. Most of the men in the other claws fought and shoved to get to the food fastest, but they learned that Squad 3-4 had the largest men, and they gave way when the squad entered the feed hall.

Owyn didn't pay much attention to the constant competition between the men in the different claws. When the claws worked together on an exercise, they tried to show each other up in front of their lieutenants, but Owyn ignored the problems. His mind was usually trying to figure out ways to get into the castle or get a message to Anna.

Some of the men took to pulling pranks on the other claws in retribution for perceived losses. If men from their den would sneak out at night, Owyn and a few others would stay behind. Owyn appreciated these brief moments of quiet to himself. He couldn't focus on the petty goings-on of these humans while trying to get his body to obey his desire to change it back to what it used to be. Occasionally he searched inside himself for the warmth and comforting sensation of fire in his belly. Unfortunately, his core stayed as cold as the day he thought he had died.

From what the men could ascertain, they would have to pass four main tests to be accepted into the army: strength, endurance, agility, and bravery. They spent long nights speculating what those tests might entail. If they failed, they would be kicked out and blacked out. Meaning they could never again attempt to join the army.

"The first three are easy enough to figure out," Addil mumbled one night, a week into their training. "But a test for bravery? What could they possibly do for that?"

"Plenty," Brandell said from his bunk while playing a dice game with Taka. "It would be easy enough to threaten to kill you and see how you handle it."

"And easy enough for us to defeat that," Taka said.

"Only if you know it's coming," Brandell bit back with a pointed finger.

"What do you mean?" Addil asked, pulling his face out of a book and turning to face Brandell.

"I play tricks on people all the time," Brandell said. "The most important element is to make sure they are comfortable and think they know what's going on."

"Misdirection," Taka nodded.

"No," Brandell said, "no direction."

"What?" Addil looked bewildered.

Brandell jumped off his bed to sit next to Addil. "Think about it," he said, "When will we be most comfortable with our training?"

"At the end," Addil said. "Before the test."

"Wrong," Brandell looked to the others expectantly.

"After the test," Maelin whispered.

Brandell clapped his hands.

"Are you suggesting," Addil adjusted his glasses, "that the real test of bravery will be to go to war with the dragons? Perhaps even just be willing to fight the dragons?"

Brandell shook his head and stood to look everyone in the eye. "I'm saying I think the war with the dragons is only a means for the test. I'm saying I think the war is a fake."

After a few moments of silence, Darwick spoke. "Why?" he asked. "Why would the king go so far as to declare war on the dragons just for a test?"

Brandell jumped back up to his bed. "Why would he declare war on the dragons? It's not like the dragons even know someone has declared war on them."

"You're right about one thing," Tua muttered. "This war doesn't make any sense."

"But at least I'll get paid to play along," Taka mumbled back.

"He's right," Nolan spoke up. "Why would the king declare war on dragons? It's like declaring war on scorrands. It doesn't make sense. Usually war is declared over an injustice. The participants feel they have or will be wronged. But how can a stupid animal feel wronged when they have no idea of our – or anyone's – motivations?"

Owyn thought back to the same arguments Rakgar had given the dragons against acting on the threat of war. Owyn realized Rakgar had been wiser than Hiro understood.

"It's just like in the history of Caluppi," Addil pointed to the book he had been reading.

"Who is Caluppi?" Owyn asked before he could stop himself.

"Caluppi," Addil picked up the book and brought it to Owyn as he spoke, "was a king in the time before the five swords brought peace. But he was wise enough not to take offense at a wrong from another kingdom. He avoided war several times by his cautious reaction to situations. You can read about it if you want."

Owyn thumbed through the pages briefly, but handed the little tome back to Addil. "I would, but I can't read."

Addil took the book back. "Is that something you've forgotten as well?"

"Not everyone gets a fine education," Darwick grunted.

"I think everyone should be able to read," Nolan sniffed. "It sets us apart from the animals."

Owyn paused at that. Could that possibly be the reason humans thought themselves better than dragons? Because dragons couldn't read?

"It makes some think they are better than others," Darwick glared through narrow eyes at Nolan.

"I'll teach you," Addil said to Darwick, then turned to Owyn. "It's not hard. I'll teach both of you."

Darwick grunted and turned his back to Addil.

"What if one of the tests includes reading?" Maelin said.

"The agility required might include having an agile mind," Tua added.

"By that way of thinking," Owyn said, quietly, "strength required could also mean strength of will." He considered the strength of will required for the Krusible, and wondered if the humans established their tests in the same way. Would he have to endure a test similar to the Krusible again? Would he be capable of passing it this time?

"Would that mean having to read one of Addil's boring books?" Brandell grumbled from his bunk. "Because I don't think anyone but Addil has either the agility or the strength for that."

Owyn thought about his place among humans. He was considered well educated for a dragon. He wouldn't want to settle for any less consideration among humans as well. If he was going to live as a human for the rest of his life, he would have to adapt. Plus, learning to read as a human could be advantageous if he ever got back to the dragons. At the very least, he could be helpful to the dragons as a human, but he might be even more valuable to them if he could read.

"I'll learn," he answered Addil. And with an evil grin at Darwick's back, he added, "And I'll do it faster than Darwick."

Darwick spun to face him and barked, "You will not!"

21

Attribution

Owyn expected the training to get easier as they went along, but it only intensified. Callum, or whichever leader was in charge of the group, would shout at the men to move faster and push themselves harder. The labor and running and lifting and weapons and fighting were not difficult for Owyn, but a few of the other men lacked the stamina required.

"He needs a rest," Thaddius shouted at Callum as he knelt beside Addil. Addil's face was pale, his lips moist from the breakfast gruel disgorging itself from his stomach. "He isn't as strong as the rest of us," Thaddius pleaded.

The men had been running around the edge of the training field while carrying large rocks. Callum had them chanting the code names used for enemies depending on species, rank, and lethality. Addil, who had been running in front of Thaddius, collapsed on the ground.

"And what will happen if he doesn't get stronger?" Callum said. His voice didn't rise. "What will happen if his strength runs out while he stands in the shadow of a dragon?"

In response, Thaddius jumped to his feet and faced the lieutenant with his fists clenched. At first Owyn thought he might hit the lieutenant. Instead, Thaddius pointed to himself. "I will be there," he whispered dangerously.

In the silence, a small voice said, "As will I." Tua stepped next to Thaddius. In turn each man, including Owyn, stepped up next to Thaddius, adding their avowal.

Callum nodded. "Good," he said. "It's noble to stand up for others and I commend you. But," he stepped closer to Thaddius and glared into his eyes. "Will you be the one to pass Addil's test of strength?"

Days and nights blurred past. Eating, running, lifting, weapons, eating, running, fighting, eating, reading, lifting, running, sleeping. Every day was the same. The routine was drilled into Owyn's head. Finally came a day before their run when Callum said, "Let's try a new route today."

The men looked at each other with wide eyes.

"A new route?" Maelin asked. They had been preparing to launch their run across the training field to the water and back with Maelin in the lead as they did every morning.

"Sure," Callum said as he unbuckled his sword belt, "I'll even go with you."

The men quickly recovered from their confusion as they watched their lieutenant jog closer to the castle.

The group hugged the castle's battlements as they ran in a tight formation. They skirted the other claws as they began their own training for the day. As they ran by Squad 7-2 pulling out their weapons, Owyn caught an angry look on one of the other men's faces.

"Sir," Maelin said, noticing the same brooding gaze from the other claw, "where are we going?"

Callum motioned for Maelin to take the lead and continue in the direction they were heading. He dropped back so he now ran alongside the three rows of three men following Maelin.

"Every training session has one group that does better than the others," he said as the men ran together. "In this training session it's Squad 3-4." The men smiled at each other and a couple clapped each other on the back. Owyn and Koris grinned at each other.

"You have every right to be proud of yourselves," Callum continued. "You've exceeded my every expectation, beginning with the first night. You have shown yourselves to be noble in every sense of the word. As a reward," he grinned, "we're running to the other side of the castle, so you can see the officer and royal training grounds."

The men whooped as they ran. Maelin picked up a little speed and all the men followed suit without thinking. They clapped each other on the shoulders and Brandell and Taka slapped hands.

Owyn grinned at Koris again, but his mind raced. This was it. This was his chance to see or talk to Anna or Philip or someone else close to them. What would he say? Would he tell them he knew Anna? Would she recognize him? Would she even be there?

"Don't get too carried away," Callum shouted. He had rejoined Maelin at the front of the claw. "Who remembers what I told you about the officer's training ground at the beginning of your training?"

"You said," Addil quoted, "'If any of you so much as glance in the direction of the castle training grounds, I'll cut you down myself.'"

"And don't think I won't do it," Callum answered. "I'll allow you to look at the training grounds around the other side of the castle but keeping your eyes where they belong will be harder than usual. You are the only group allowed to visit the grounds because I know I can trust you to do as you're told.

"There will be women out on the training grounds," he continued, "which often includes the princess. The king has allowed the women to train with swords. You are not to even look in their direction. If you see them, immediately look away. We will not run anywhere near where they train, so avoiding contact with your eyes shouldn't be all that difficult. I will allow you to take in the officer's outdoor training grounds and the training grounds under the castle. If the king or royal general are present, you will lower your eyes to the ground and keep them there. If I have to remind anyone, there will be consequences."

The group ran in silence. Owyn's mind reeled. What would he do if Anna were there? How could he speak to her? He would be surrounded by armed men. He could endanger Koris and their entire claw if he made a wrong move.

What does it matter? he chided himself. *You're a dragon. They're only humans.*

He looked down at his legs as they pumped under him. He felt every pounding footfall. He felt his blood coursing through his body. He looked at the men around him. Koris, who had helped and supported him. Someone he had come to look upon as a friend. Addil, who had taught him to read. Thaddius, who would willingly give up his position as a fighter because he admitted Owyn was stronger. Brandell and Taka, who had become like brothers to each other and the men in the claw. They had taken the playful role of Prak in Owyn's life. Could he really betray these men? They had bled and sweated alongside each other. They had prevailed and flourished beside each other. They trusted him. Did he trust them?

Before long the group circled around the side of the castle closest to Teardrop Sea. They could see the King's Forest below the mountains. Stretching before them was a large open area. There were stables nearby, closer to the front side of the castle. Next to the stables, closer to the forest and farthest from Teardrop Sea, Owyn could just make out a group of women clad in black from head to toe. The women swung small swords in unison. The group looked similar to the mouth of a dragon, with many teeth.

"It appears," Callum said to the group, "the princess is present today." He turned to run backward so he was looking at the men. "If you look to your left," he indicated with his hand, guiding all their eyes away from the women in black, "you'll see where the generals practice with their swords."

Owyn allowed his eyes to drift, following Callum's indication. The claw could see several officers swinging swords alone, but many of them were paired. They wore little armor, but swung the swords so hard Owyn could hear the clashes.

"Isn't that dangerous?" Tua echoed Owyn's thoughts. "Won't they hurt each other if they spar without armor?"

"The practice swords are blunt," Callum answered. "Besides the fact they are very adept, especially when it comes to control."

The men watched the senior officers swinging the swords as they loped by. Callum pointed out things of interest. The target range. The staff throw range. The fighting ring. Apparently the king and royal general weren't present, so they could look wherever they wanted. He pointed out the stables but turned the group away well before they reached them. Swinging the group in a wide arc, the claw headed back toward Teardrop Sea. Callum hadn't lied, he'd kept them well clear of the women.

Last chance, Owyn thought as the group curved around the training area.

Even keeping his head down as instructed, Owyn could still see the women as they swung their swords. Three women paced around the perimeter of the group, calling out orders. Of their own accord, Owyn's eyes crept toward the sound.

The first woman he saw was much larger than Anna. Not in height, for Anna could rival most men in height, but in build. The woman looked strong, as if she could break even Owyn in half. Then Anna stepped out from behind her. Even from this distance he recognized her immediately. Her blonde hair blew in the light breeze. Especially with the black dress and leather bucklers, she looked more fierce and fearless than ever.

Anna glanced at the men running past. Owyn's heart stopped as her eyes passed over him, then returned to meet his. The piercing green of hers stabbed into his. Yes, he still loved her. He had to go to her. He had to do something. Even if it meant betraying the men that trusted him.

"Drop your eyes!" said a whisper that sounded like anything but. Callum's face loomed in front of Owyn's. Only because Owyn still held his head angled down was Callum able to place his nose within a breath of Owyn's. "Don't make me kill you, guard." The lieutenant said it low, but there was no mistaking the truth of the threat. Even for a new human like Owyn.

Owyn dropped his eyes. If he was going to disobey and speak to Anna, he wouldn't be able to do it now. Koris tugged at his arm. Callum shoved his head down to the ground. "You will run with your face in the mud until you get to your den. Then I don't want to see your face until tomorrow at your trials."

Philip examined scorch marks over some of the ground and a large boulder on the perimeter of the camp.

"The men have done well rebuilding," Torgon pointed to the newly built cabins nestled in the canyon. "The camp looks much like it did when I first came here, except that everything is newer."

The royal party had arrived only the night before. After sleeping as much as he could, Philip had awakened early that morning to receive reports from the captain stationed here at the halfway point to the Great Northern Mountain, and to search the area on his own.

"We can't stay for any more rest, you know," Philip stood, brushing soot from his gloves.

Torgon nodded. "I've already told the men we'll be leaving shortly. The only question is about which direction we'll go."

"I know we had originally planned to go all the way north, but the dragon attack put us off schedule." Philip hesitated to make a decision. He had planned on going to the Great Northern Mountain to check on production of the dragon poison and arrows. When this facility had originally been destroyed, most of the poison produced had been destroyed with it. Now

Murzod had the men working tirelessly to replace the stockpiles and send them here.

"I know," Torgon sighed with mock sincerity, "I was looking forward to seeing Murzod again too. I just miss him so much."

Philip couldn't help but grin. "As much as I had hoped he'd attend the wedding," he said, jokingly, "I think it's more important for me to be there."

"The rest of the army is well on their way to the Rock Clouds," Torgon said. "The other kingdoms are almost there as well. We need to join them before they start the fighting without us. As it is, many groups are being attacked by centaurs. We think the centaurs are probably protecting the dragons. It might be dangerous for us to continue."

Philip nodded. "Then it's settled," he said. "We'll go back to Kingstor to finalize the marriage—"

"—whether Anna or Dieko likes it or not—" Torgon interjected.

"—then we'll go to the Great Northern Mountain after the wedding," Philip said. "We'll inspect it and see what needs to be done there, then take a shipment of the poison with us to the Rock Clouds. If we use the faeries' concoction, we should move fairly quickly."

Torgon nodded, inspecting his boots. "Will we be bringing the princess with us?"

Philip sighed. "Once she's married, I don't see that we'll have much choice. She'll have earned the right to know the plans and Dieko will need to see and learn everything as well."

"Not exactly the post-wedding tradition," Torgon mumbled.

"Not what worries me," Philip answered. Without looking at his friend, Philip's eyes drifted in the direction of Kingstor Noble. "I'm only afraid of who else Anna will insist on bringing with her."

22

Requite

"Your first trial," Callum shouted over the men in Squad 3-4, "is a test of endurance."

The ten men stood at the water's edge. Callum had allowed them to eat breakfast, but instead of going on their customary morning run, he told them to run down to the water's edge and choose a rock from the pile nearby. He proceeded to walk down slowly after them, allowing them time to choose a rock. When he reached them, he told them to hold the rocks over their heads.

The men now stood within in a few inches of the lapping sea water, holding the rocks over their heads. Callum pulled out an apple and a knife. Sitting on the pile of rocks, he cut large chunks out of it, slowly munching on each bite.

"Brandell," Callum said after a bite of his apple, "who would you say is the leader of your claw?"

Brandell shrugged as much as he could while holding his rock. "Maelin," he said without hesitation. Maelin said nothing.

"Tua," the lieutenant said, "would you agree?"

"Yes," Tua answered. Again without any hesitation.

He indicated all of the men without saying any names, "All of you would agree?"

They all either nodded their heads or answered in the affirmative. Callum nodded, taking another bite of his apple.

"Normally," he said after a moment, "lieutenants have to assign a leader to new claws. Especially if they can't agree on someone within their ranks. Squad 7-2," he indicated the group of men further up the field that seemed to be using their wooden weapons to spar with their lieutenant, "almost came to blows over who should be their leader." He chuckled as he cut into his apple again, shaking his head. "And here you men did it without realizing or being asked."

Callum finished his apple and lay on the beach with his hands behind his head. He spoke to the men about their training, about each other, about what they wanted to do both while they were in the army, and later in life. He questioned them on the things they had learned during training.

Before long, Addil's arms began to quake. He had chosen the smallest of the rocks. He always had while training. And although he had gotten much stronger, he still struggled to match the other men. Even Taka, as slight of build as Addil, had unusually large reserves of strength.

"I don't know if I can do it," Addil whispered to Thaddius next to him. Owyn could hear him with his sensitive hearing.

"You can do this," Thaddius encouraged.

"I can't," Addil insisted. "I'm just not as strong as you." His arms shook. When he adjusted the rock in his hands, his legs shook.

"How much longer will we have to hold these?" Thaddius asked Callum.

Callum looked toward the horizon. Shielding his eyes from its rays, he pointed at the sun rising high over the water. "Two hands," he said, "we're only at one."

Two hands. Owyn's arms had begun to ache, but he shifted the weight of the rock between his two hands, resting one at a time, but not removing either hand. He had watched Addil do this early in the exercise, but it wasn't doing him any good now.

Every eye was on Addil. Owyn could see Thaddius's face. His eyes pled with Addil to keep the rock above his head.

"What happens," Thaddius asked in a shaky voice, "if we drop the rock?"

Callum looked at him and stared.

"Can we put it on our heads?" Brandell asked. "It will still be over our heads and our hands still on it."

Callum shook his head.

"I can't do it," Addil's face dripped with sweat. His arms shook violently.

"You have to," Thaddius insisted.

"You can do this, Addil," Tua said.

Everyone offered words of encouragement, except Thaddius, whose mind seemed to be grinding at the possibility of losing a man.

"I'm sorry," Addil looked into Thaddius's eyes, "it seems you will have to continue without me."

"No!" Thaddius snapped. "Who will be our idea man?"

Tears joined the sweat rolling down Addil's cheeks. Owyn's chest compressed watching the small man. He wanted to help him. He couldn't help but feel that Addil's mind and heart were a hundred times stronger than his own. How had these men created such a hold on him so quickly? They were resourceful, strong, brave, and not nearly as brutal as he had been taught in his previous life.

"Wait," Thaddius's head jerked up to look at Callum, "do we have to stand on our feet?"

Callum scowled. "What do you mean?"

"Can I hold the rock above my head while I kneel on the ground?" Thaddius said.

Callum considered for a moment, his eyes bouncing between the two men. After what seemed an eternity, he shrugged. "I suppose you can."

"Hold on," Thaddius said to Addil. He walked around behind the smaller man. Kneeling behind Addil, Thaddius was careful to keep his rock above his head.

Once on his knees, the top of Thaddius's rock reached the same height as the bottom of Addil's. "Tilt your rock back, slowly," he whispered.

"Now wait just a second," Callum started to protest, but Maelin and Nolan took a step forward.

"They're following the rules as you explained them," Nolan stated.

"They're each still holding their rocks," Maelin indicated.

Slowly, Addil tipped his rock behind him. The rocks gently bumped together. Addil's shoulders relaxed. He didn't remove his hands from the rock, but his arms slowly stopped shaking. Tears flowed down his face in earnest.

Callum sighed. "I suppose they aren't technically breaking any rules."

Once Callum finally called an end to the endurance test, the rocks were dropped in the water not to be retrieved. Callum allowed the men a short break to massage tired muscles and drink from their water skins. Owyn sat quietly in the sand, allowing the surf to wash over his bare feet. No one stopped Thaddius from lying on the ground. Addil fetched his water skin for him.

After their rest, Callum told the men to follow him. He led them up the field to the weapons.

"Agility," Callum said, "can mean several things. In this instance I will test your agility with weapons." He chose a long stick meant to simulate a sword and swung it in large circles at his side. "For this test, I will be your opponent. Although you are not technically being tested with your sword, I wish to see what handling skills you have learned and can capably perform. Who will be first?"

The men looked at each other, every one of them tired and barely able to lift their arms after the grueling endurance test. Thaddius didn't look up.

"I will," Maelin finally stepped forward. He chose a stick and swung it in lazy circles.

"You really are the leader, aren't you?" Callum said.

Maelin shrugged.

Callum swung the sword at each man in turn but didn't seem to be doing all he could. Maelin did passing well, according to Callum. Then Tua and Koris took their turns. Each man was easily disarmed or swatted with the unforgiving stick wielded by their lieutenant. But each received positive remarks from the lieutenant when they finished.

Nolan handily did the best. He had received early sword training when he was young, but was forced to stop by a father who insisted he wouldn't have any need to defend himself. Darwick, Brandell, and Addil were disarmed before they knew what was going on. Callum allowed them all a second try, but it was obvious to the group they would all have to work a lot harder on the sword if they ever wanted to be promoted.

"Well done, Taka," Callum said after he had disarmed the man. "I have a feeling you don't need a sword to defeat an opponent. Who's next?"

"Owyn," Maelin said.

Owyn stood and took the stick Taka proffered him. Callum hadn't met his eyes or spoken to Owyn that day. He saw the lieutenant's jaw clench when Maelin said his name.

Without meeting his eyes, Callum pointed his stick at Owyn. "You," he said in a dangerous, low voice, "are lucky you're still here to be tested."

When Callum's eyes finally lifted to his, Owyn could see the lingering anger from the previous day's royal run-in. Owyn nodded, lifting his weapon. He had no excuse. He had considered abandoning the men. He had considered abandoning everything. He was willing to do it again.

Callum swung his stick harder at Owyn than Owyn had seen him do at any of the other men. The anger Callum had been withholding surfaced on his face as he fought the larger man. Owyn's dragon senses kicked in. He blocked and countered smoothly, only to meet Callum's weapon time and time again. Callum pressed Owyn further, moving his stick in huge arcs, then slicing in at an unforeseen angle. Owyn could see every detail of the other man, his dragon sight catching every movement of the man's muscles. He could hear the lieutenant's heart pounding faster as Owyn sliced his stick toward him. Owyn felt that swinging his stick by instinct came to him as easily as sneaking through the forest as a dragon without making a sound. Just as measured. Just as slow.

Suddenly, the burning fire in Owyn's belly blazed. It felt uncomfortably hot. Hotter than it had felt thus far as a human. His focus shifting to the flame in his middle, his weapon slowed. Callum swung his stick in a circle, then cut down sharply with his hand almost against Owyn's. The maneuver yanked Owyn's weapon out of his hand.

Silence swallowed the group as the stick clattered to the ground. Pursing his lips, Callum scooped the stick from the ground and stepped up to Owyn. He glared up at Owyn.

Callum turned to the rest of the men. "Go get your mid-day meal," he said. "Meet me at the lifting station when you're done."

"But sir," Maelin said, "Thaddius hasn't been tested."

Callum looked down on Thaddius. Thaddius nodded his head. "I'm ready," he said, but when he tried to push himself off the ground, his arms shook and he collapsed again.

"You're a fighter," Callum said. "You'll have no need of a sword in the army. I consider your test passed."

The men began to walk away, Addil and Maelin on either side supporting Thaddius, congratulating each other and ready for a meal. Before Owyn could follow them, Callum grabbed him by the arm.

"If you can decide who is worthy of your fealty," the lieutenant growled low in his ear, "you might be worthy to serve them."

After the mid-day meal, the trial of strength started at the rock pile. Callum told the men to divide the rocks into groups, one group for each man. Then they had to move the entire pile across the training field.

"That's easy," Brandell sneered.

"But you can only make one trip," Callum clarified.

The men worked together, piling rocks on the largest men. With Addil directing the piles and who should carry them, and who should support those carrying, the group moved slowly across the field.

"That was the fastest any group has passed this test today," Callum congratulated them as they dumped the rocks on the other side of the training field.

Owyn and Thaddius, who had shared the bulk of the weight, hunched over their knees, breathing hard and fast. Sweat rolled freely down their faces. Owyn's knees shook as he tried to remain upright.

"That was...definitely...not..." Owyn panted, "...a test...of strength...of will."

Addil slapped the two big men on the back. As the men congratulated each other, Callum waited for the noise to die down.

"You only have one test left," he announced to the men. "Courage."

The men eyed each other and their lieutenant. Some grinned. Others looked wary. Maelin squinted at Callum.

"Unfortunately," Callum told the group, "you will have to wait for sundown to complete the task. Meet me then, on the beach next to the King's Forest. Bring your weapons."

23

Courage

That evening the men from Squad 3-4 walked along the beach behind the castle. Each man carried the staff they'd been given. All of the men smiled as they sauntered along the beach. Owyn could feel the eyes of the guards in the towers making sure the men didn't wander any closer to the castle ground than allowed.

"Can you imagine the trouble we could get into up there?" Brandell muttered conspiratorially to Taka.

"Don't tell me you wish to be assigned to the castle?" Tua accused.

Taka shrugged. "It might be fun."

"Nah," Brandell said, "we'd have to behave!"

The group continued small chatter as they made their way further behind the King's Forest along the beach. So far, there was no sign of Callum as the sun dipped behind the trees.

Maelin scanned the beach, wondering aloud where the lieutenant might be, when Owyn spotted him walking toward them from the direction of the mountains.

Once Callum joined them, he turned to walk back toward the mountains where they joined the sea beyond the King's Forest. He beckoned the men to follow him, but said nothing about where they were going or what they would be doing. He walked with his head facing the ground and his hands clasped behind his back.

Well after the sun had set they finally reached the bottom of the cliff. The night was warm enough to be comfortable and stars sparkled in the sky. The three moons of Avonoa rose in three small slivers over the water.

The beach ended abruptly, the sand turning to mountainous piles of boulders. The sharp edges and jagged peaks reminded Owyn that those boulders continued long down the edge of Teardrop Sea. Callum stopped at the base of a sheer cliff and spun to face the men with the boulders at his back.

Next to the lieutenant a torch burned, held aloft by a metal staff planted in the sand. More unlit torches lay on the ground next to it. Next to those, a small opening yawned at the base of the cliff. Darkness seemed to sink away into an opening barely large enough for a man to squeeze through.

"This," Callum said, indicating the cave opening, "is your next task."

As if by design, an echoing roar sounded from the cave. The men from Squad 3-4 shied away from the cave.

"What is that?" Darwick whispered.

"That," Callum paused to stare into the eyes of the men in front of him, "is a dragon."

A dragon. Owyn's mind reeled. A dragon. A real dragon. He hadn't heard of anyone going missing, but it could have been anyone, from any ruck. With so many dragons dying recently or being killed, someone could have easily gone missing.

"No one knows how it got in there," Callum continued, "but it's grown too large to escape. The guards above us found it several years ago."

"What guards?" Nolan asked.

"There are guards posted on the cliffside," Callum said. "While most of the kingdom and army believe their main job is to watch for danger from across the water, they also keep this beast alive."

Alive? Keep it alive? Owyn's mind raced. If a dragon was trapped in that cave it could have been sent there as a punishment. The dragon might have been sentenced to death. It should be dead. The humans had no idea they might be harboring a criminal.

"How do they do that?" Addil asked.

"What do you mean, how?" Koris growled. "Why?"

Callum grinned. "By order of the king's majishun, Travaith. He studies the monster. Tries to gather majikal ingredients, as I understand it. In return for the guards keeping it alive, he allows us to use it for this trial."

Owyn's head spun. What if he could talk to whoever it was in that cave? What if he could free them? Perhaps, at the very least, the dragon in the cave could get word to the other dragons that Philip is going to attack the Rock Clouds. On the other hand, if it was a criminal in there, did he want to free them? Would they even be willing to help? They might be penitent enough from the treatment of the humans that they would be willing to assist Owyn. There had to be some way to figure out if he could help whoever it was in the cave. There had to be something he could do!

"Do you want us to kill it?" Thaddius said, eyeing the cave as if deciding his plan of attack.

"Or try?" Tua said in a small voice.

"By Tartaku," Callum exclaimed, "no! Travaith would never forgive me! No," he waved a hand at the cave opening, "the dragon has a stash of gold. Your task will be to extract pieces of it. A piece of gold for every man. And you must go in one at a time." He eyed Thaddius and Addil.

"Steal from a dragon?!" Taka looked pale in the moonlight.

"Are you mad?" Tua's eyes stared wild at Callum.

Thaddius glanced between Callum and the cave. Addil looked like he was going to be sick.

"I'll go." The words left Owyn's lips almost before they'd formed in his mind. He had to get into that cave and he had to do it before anyone else could anger the dragon.

"Are you crazy?" Koris whispered. "You just survived a dragon attack."

"Exactly," Owyn said. "I'm the only one qualified."

Callum nodded with a half-grin. "You might even survive," he said.

"No one has survived?" Brandell whimpered.

"Why would you send us in there?" Taka said.

"Well," Callum amended, "men do survive. A few of them even come out without injury. It's just, well," he looked up at Owyn, "it's usually the larger men that don't come out again."

"No," Maelin said suddenly. "I'm the leader. I should go first."

"Wait a second," Darwick said, "should any of us be going in there? It doesn't seem safe."

"Darwick's right," Addil said, swallowing hard. "Perhaps I should go first. The smaller men might be able to hide themselves better. That's why more of them survive."

Another roar echoed from the cave, louder than the first.

"Hmm," Callum said, as if to himself. "When he roars more often, it means he's hungry."

The men fell silent.

Owyn clenched his jaw. He had to get in there. "I'll be fine," he grumbled. He stepped over to the unlit torches. Lighting a torch for himself, he walked toward the cave opening, but Callum called to him again.

"You're allowed to take your staff, but," he indicated Owyn's belt buckle and pouch, "not anything shiny."

Owyn knew the rumor that if humans gave something shiny to a dragon in order to spare their lives wasn't true. If humans gave a dragon something shiny, it would give the dragon an excuse to leave and not harm the human. Other than that, dragons didn't eat humans. Maim or kill, sure. If they had cause. But eat? Never.

"You'll each have to go all the way through the cave," Callum continued. "Emerge at the other end of the cave with a piece of gold from the hoard, and you pass your trial. We'll regroup there."

Owyn nodded and handed over his belt and the pouch. Then, giving the group of men one last nod, he slipped into the cave.

He had to duck to get through the opening. The walls were so close together he had to squeeze through a few spots. He understood why a fully-grown dragon wouldn't be able to get out of the cave again. Especially a male.

Owyn held the torch in front of him at arm's length, attempting to light his path. He hoped that if he put the fire in front of himself the dragon would see it more as an offering than a threat. Of course, he could try to blow the fire in front of him to make the dragon think he was another dragon, but another dragon would never fit through that opening, no matter how the first one got there.

As he moved through the cave, the stifling passageway opened up to allow a little more space to walk. The passageway meandered back and forth with many curves and twists, deeper and deeper under the mountain.

Owyn began to wonder if he was still moving in the right direction. He stopped and looked around him. Although hidden dark spots evaded his torchlight, he didn't see anything that looked like another trail to follow. While he searched to make sure he was on the right path, roars echoed from ahead. The roars grew louder.

Picking up his pace, Owyn ran through the tunnels. It was much further to reach the noise than he thought possible. Rocks reached from the walls to scratch at his arms as he ran ahead of his torchlight. Finally, he heard a deafening roar. He must be only steps away from the dragon.

"Who's there?" Owyn whispered into the dark. "Who are you?"

Silence.

"It's alright," he said, inching his way around a curve in the cave wall. "I'm a friend. I can help you."

Nothing.

"I promise," he persisted. He'd been thinking of a way to get the dragon to trust him. "I know you can speak. I want to help you. Tell me who you are. What ruck are you from? I'll help you escape. I'll get others to help as well."

He heard movement, sound ricocheting wildly off the cave walls around a corner in front of him.

"Please," he said, keeping his voice low in case any of the other men had entered the cave behind him.

"I won't tell anyone you spoke to me." More movement around the corner. "I know you can understand me. You don't have to pretend. You're safe. I'm going to help you."

The movement around the corner slowed. Something scuffed the rock on the other side of the barrier. Owyn knew the dragon had no reason to trust him. He knew exactly what the dragon would be thinking, even if he were a criminal and an outcast. But Owyn had to try.

"I'm coming around now," Owyn said. He kept his voice low and steady, as Adair had when he first met Owyn in the forest. He felt no fear. He hoped the dragon could sense his calm as well.

Stepping around the corner, Owyn's torch immediately flew from his hand. A human hand clamped over his mouth and dragged him to the ground. Before Owyn could wrestle the hand away from his face, in the light of his torch he saw a man's boots step past him into the passageway he had just been pulled from.

Owyn tugged at the hand over his mouth. The owner's face appeared next to Owyn's head with a grin on it. A second man held his hands up in front of Owyn. Several men stood behind the man covering Owyn's mouth. They all wore the blue tunic of the guards of the Noble Kingdom. The man whose hands were in front of Owyn put a single finger against his own lips.

As Owyn's tensed muscles relaxed, the man with his hand over Owyn's mouth loosened his grip, but didn't release it. All the men in the cave turned toward the man who had taken Owyn's place in the passageway. In one hand, that man held a hardened leather ball with a large opening in the front and placed it in front of his mouth. He held up three fingers with the other hand, then two, then one. When he removed the last finger, he grabbed the ball and screamed into it. At the same time, all of the men yelled and the man restraining Owyn removed his hand.

The sound of all of the men together made the roaring Owyn and the others had heard.

"Sorry if we scared you," a man whispered.

"No, we're not," another whispered back with a chuckle.

"Taming," another said as he guided Owyn back to his torch, which had been ripped from his hand by yet another man. "I tried taming too. Although I hadn't thought about telling the dragon I knew it could speak. That's original."

He gave Owyn his torch and sent him toward another man. "It's a rite of passage," the next man said. "There are a few other ways to get into the army, but if you're lucky enough to get this one, we call ourselves cavers."

Another man stepped forward to guide Owyn through the rest of the cave. Talking to him through the rest of the caverns toward the exit, he explained that the bravery test was to see if men would go into a cave with a dragon. He explained that no one was allowed to ever tell anyone of the experience or they would be blacked out and shunned.

They stepped out of the cavern into the dark trees of the King's Forest and the other Noble guards waiting outside told him the rest of his claw would join him soon. As they recounted their own tales of having been through the dragon cave the first time, Owyn's heart dropped. He realized the fire in his belly sputtered out again.

One at a time, the rest of the men from Squad 3-4 joined Owyn and the guards at the exit to the cave. Brandell was easily the most vocal about his experience. Tua came through the exit with his face as white as the moons' faces. Even Thaddius looked visibly shaken exiting the caverns.

As the men recovered, the guards pulled out casks of ale and passed around cups in celebration. Callum eventually joined them, following Darwick through last.

"I'm very proud of all of you," Callum announced to the large gathering. "A finer training group has never graduated into the service of the king. Except, perhaps, my claw." To this a few of the guards cheered and some of them booed.

Callum waved his hands to calm them all. "Unfortunately," he said mainly to the men of 3-4, "none of you failed your trials."

"What?" a man said from the side.

"What do you mean?" another man said, standing up next to Callum. "None of them failed?"

Callum nodded. The other man shook his head. A grave shadow moved over his face as he sat back on the ground next to the other guards.

"Why?" Brandell asked. "What's wrong with all of us passing?"

"You're not all allowed to pass," the man said from his seat on the ground. But Callum waved away his comment.

"Not every man in a training claw is allowed to pass," Callum told 3-4. "Someone must fail."

"Why?" Maelin said.

"That's hardly fair," Thaddius growled.

"The trials must weed out the weakest men," Callum said with a firm tone. "That's why they're made to be so difficult." His gaze rested on Addil.

Addil met the lieutenant's eye. "I have to fail," he whispered.

"No," Callum said, "I'm going to allow your claw to choose. You can choose to see Addil go home, or," he said, turning to the rest of the claw, "you could consider Thaddius, because he didn't test for agility or any one of you. You can choose or volunteer anyone, but someone must go home. Never to return."

The men searched each other's faces. They'd spent weeks training together, supporting each other as everyone passed the trials. How could they possibly reject one? Owyn knew he should offer to go. He had no reason to be in the army and besides, he was supposed to hate humans. Well, except for the one he loved. And perhaps he could have been friends with these men.

They had exceeded his expectations of humans. But he knew he didn't really belong.

"I'll go," he said, quietly.

"No," Addil snapped. "I failed. I never would have passed the strength trial without Thaddius."

The other guards waited. Quietly. Their faces unreadable.

Thaddius glared at the ground.

"It's ok," Addil said, laying a hand on Thaddius's arm. "I don't really belong here anyway."

"But you're the idea man," Brandell muttered.

"No," Addil said. He placed his cup on the ground and stood. Dusting his pants, he straightened his back and stood tall. Taller than Owyn had ever seen him stand before. "This is the way it needs to be. If anyone will be protecting the kingdom, it should be the rest of you."

"No," Thaddius said. Addil opened his mouth to argue, but Thaddius said it again, louder, "No!" Thaddius stood up next to Addil. "I won't serve this kingdom if they are willing to waste the talent of men like Addil. No. If he goes, I go." He glared at Callum, daring him to argue.

"Me too," Maelin said. "I am the leader of this claw and I won't serve unless all of my men serve with me."

"Us too!" Brandell and Taka yelled at the same time while jumping to their feet.

Owyn joined as every man in Squad 3-4 stood next to each other.

Darwick slowly stood last and stepped in front of Addil to face Callum. "Tis noble to feel the burden of fate, but nobler still to feel the burdens of others."

"Darwick," Callum grinned, "are you quoting Shantari's Prophecies and Praises of Shurka?"

"Addil taught me to read," the bearded man growled at the officer.

Callum nodded. "And Shantari is correct," he said. "This final trial was a test of nobility."

The claw looked around at the other men in the forest as each one lifted a cup to them. When their eyes returned to Callum, he lifted a cup as well. "And you all passed."

24

Disgusting

"Well," Koris said, "we did it." He clapped Owyn on the shoulder as he and the other men packed their belongings. They would be moving into the regular army barracks after the swearing ceremony. Once they swore their fealty to the crown of the Noble Kingdom, they would receive their assignments. Every one of the men in Squad 3-4 believed they would be leaving in the next group to join the army at the Rock Clouds. The order only had to be issued.

Owyn watched the men as they gathered their things. They joked with each other, laughed, and spoke of the great deeds they would do in the war. They all had plans to show how noble they were and how much they deserved greatness. Nolan's family had plenty of wealth and power, so he planned on testing for promotion to lieutenant soon enough. He claimed he would request Squad 3-4 to be assigned to him.

The men stashed their bags with those of the other claws, reluctantly setting them down beside the belongings of Squad 7-2. All four claws waited in the same area. Many men chatted and congratulated each other on their success. Some commiserated that a few men had been failed and therefore denied the chance to ever join the Noble Army.

Finally, General Tommak marched into the training courtyard with two captains in tow.

"Join your squads," the general shouted.

The men scurried into their groups. Only Squad 3-4 had a previously conceived formation and they fell in faster than the other claws did. Tommak acknowledged their order and asked everyone to follow their lead. The claws finally each shifted into three rows of three with their leader in front.

"You will not speak until you are told to do so, and you will be told what to say," Tommak said to the group. "You will not move unless you are told to do so, and you will be told where to move. You will not look anywhere you are not invited to, we are not on a field trip. If you so much as breathe without being told to do so, you will answer to me."

The lieutenants in charge of each squad walked in a row of four relative to their squads. Squad 3-4 marched on the far left. Owyn always fell in the middle of the back row. Maelin claimed that in most situations it would be best to have a tall man overlooking the others, to watch for danger. So Owyn marched along with no one but Koris on his left, Thaddius on his right, and no one would walk behind him.

Could I slip away? he thought to himself. *Should I risk leaving the formation once we're inside the castle grounds?*

Glancing briefly to his left and right and watching the men in front of him, he knew he couldn't do it. Not only would he betray the men, but he would have all the claws after him in moments. He knew he had to try to get to Anna, but he had to wait for the right moment.

Tommak, flanked by his captains, led the group into the castle grounds. To Owyn's horror, he led the men to the very courtyard where Hiro had been held captive for weeks during the past winter. Owyn had no problem keeping his eyes on the men in front of him. He saw the men in front of him taking short glances at the majestic courtyard surrounded by columns and open-air hallways. Owyn didn't look up. He had no desire to see the confining merlons curved like claws to keep dragons from landing on them. He knew that if he looked at them he would feel the same sense of incarceration he had felt then.

Tommak ordered the men to stay in formation. He ordered them onto the grass facing the castle keep. Above them, the king's balcony extended over them. Owyn wondered briefly if the king would use the balcony to address them.

Tommak ordered the men to take a knee. As a group, they knelt on the grass, with their hands resting on the propped leg.

"I have word," Tommak said in a low voice but loud enough for everyone to hear, "King Philip is still away. Princess Anna will be accepting your fealty to the crown today." He paused, searching the eyes of the men. Owyn's heart fluttered and raced. This was it. This was the moment. Owyn saw a few heads in front of him twitch, some breath was sucked in and many men sat up straighter, but no one spoke.

"Good," Tommak continued, "you know your place. Continue to do your duty. Princess Anna will address the group first. Then, standing on ceremony, she will ask you three questions to gauge your fealty. You will answer 'We so swear' to the first two and 'We freely give it' to the last question. Any questions?"

He searched the eyes of the men in front of him, then stepped to the side of the group as guards began filing into the courtyard from a side door. The guards, about fifteen of them, surrounded the squads kneeling on the ground. Owyn clenched his teeth. This was it. His only and last chance.

After the guards surrounded the group, they stood with their staffs at their side. Anna strode into the courtyard, flanked by two lieutenants. As she glid into the sunlight, her yellow hair wafted on a breeze. Although he couldn't smell it, Owyn remembered perfectly her light scent. His heart ached.

"Good morning," Anna said, a small smile playing on her lips. "I understand you men might have been trained never to look a royal or noble in the eye." Crossing her arms at her chest, she said, "However, you will disobey that order, if it was taught to you, and forget it. I want every single man in the courtyard to look me in the eye this moment."

Owyn saw the guards at the side snap their heads toward Anna. He had already been looking directly into Anna's eyes. Gradually, men lifted their heads. Nolan was first in their group to look up, but no one else would follow until they saw Maelin lift his gaze too.

"That's better," Anna continued. "I will not have noble guards subservient to anyone. You are all noble. I have heard wonderful things about the men who trained in this group. I would be proud to have any one of you protecting me. But first, I'm going to give you a choice."

The men glanced at one another. Even Tommak, who had been standing to the side with his arms crossed while watching the men, dropped his hands to his sides as he looked at Anna in question.

"Yes, Tommak," Anna waved him away without looking at him. "I want to make sure these men, and every man that serves in the army, does so of their own free will. I know the words you're about to recite say just this, but I want to give you the choice. Unfettered."

She paced in front of the men, looking directly into the eyes of most of them. She was close enough to the lieutenants that they could have reached out and brushed the skirts of her dress. "I don't want any man in the army," Anna continued, "to have any reservations, whatsoever, about why they serve. I want to know if you have any questions, doubts, or concerns about Philip or me, or anything we might order you to do. If any of you, for any reason, harbor doubts as to the leadership of this kingdom, please speak now. If you feel you cannot serve my brother or me for any reason, please stand up."

She watched with anticipation, her eyes almost willing someone to stand. Owyn's heart hammered in his chest. Should he speak? What would he say? How could he get some kind of message to her? Here? In front of everyone? How could he tell her he used to be a dragon? How could he profess his love for her? How could he stand now, betray everyone here he'd come to know, and yet tell her what really mattered? What could he say to explain?

Before he could answer any of the questions racing through his mind, he leapt to his feet. While searching the faces of the men in front of her, Anna had not once made eye contact with Owyn. He knew if he didn't do this now, she would never even notice him among the others. He had to do something.

"What are you doing?" Thaddius whispered harshly.

"Owyn," Koris said, tugging on his arm, "sit down."

The men in Owyn's claw turned to face him when Anna's eyes finally fell on him. She looked mildly surprised, but her shoulders relaxed.

Koris jerked harder on Owyn's arm and Thaddius joined him, almost ripping Owyn's arm from his socket. His claw coaxed him to sit, questioning his sanity.

"No," Anna waved to the men, as the other claws joined in berating him, "you must not chastise him. He stands for what he believes. Come, what is your name?"

"Owyn," he said, his heart still hammering as Thaddius and Koris ceased trying to tear his arms off.

"You'll never be forgiven for this," Thaddius whispered.

"Tell me, Owyn," Anna said, loud enough for everyone to hear, "why is it you feel you cannot serve the Noble Kingdom?"

Anna's eyes bore into him. The men waited. What could he say?

Maelin whispered "Apologize!" under his breath.

How? Owyn thought. How to get her to understand? *This is my last chance.*

"Tell her you're a crazy man," Koris said as low as Maelin had. "Apologize!"

"I..." Owyn stammered. "I can't..." He couldn't think straight. He knew his time in the army would end at this moment, but he didn't care. If he was truly stuck being a human, he had to get some kind of message to the only human who truly mattered to him. If he had to live this horrible, disgusting existence, he had to do something. Then an idea struck him. But what would happen to him if he said it?

"Yes?" Anna said, "Why do you feel you can't serve my brother or me?"

"Because," he paused, steeling himself for the onslaught of persecution. He rolled his shoulder and looked directly into Anna's beautiful eyes, willing her to understand. "Because you're disgusting."

Owyn barely saw Anna's lips part and her eyes widen before a sudden pain in his head forced darkness to overtake him.

25

Visitors

Gradually he sensed the world around him return to his consciousness, but he kept his eyes closed.

Listen for danger. Feel where you are. He had been raised to do these things since his hatching. He felt hard stone under him. Was he back in his cave? Was it all a horrible nightmare? His head hurt. The left side, next to his eye. Why did his head hurt?

Did someone hit me? he thought. *Wrong question.*

He felt the stone under him again. He was cold. Perhaps he had died and gone to the World of Souls. No, his front shoulders hurt too. He felt something around his wrists. Cold. Metal. The only sounds he heard were of water dripping and distant moaning. Soft heartbeats, very few and far away. He was safe. Somewhat.

Slowly, he opened his eyes, blinking against the pain in his head. In front of his face, his hands—*yes, hands*—were shackled together at the wrists. He still wore boots on his feet, breeches on his legs, and a shirt on his back.

Still human, he thought, laying his head back against the stone.

Once he accepted the fact, Owyn took in his surroundings. He lay against a rough, dirty stone wall. The floor and other walls were made of the same material. A broken bucket sat across the small space from hay strewn in the corner. Metal bars caked in grime blocked his view of the only distant light off to his right. He thought he could see on the other side of the bars the same kind of rough stone wall as the one he was leaning against. He could almost reach the bars with his feet. From what he could discern about the size of this enclosure, he wouldn't have been able to lay his body straight on the floor in any direction. He forced himself to ignore the dark patches on the floor and the walls lining it. He couldn't imagine how the disgusting humans around him could live in such conditions.

Then it hit him. "Disgusting." That was the word he'd said to Anna. In front of forty men willing to pledge their lives to protect her. What had he done? The men would never forgive him, not to mention Anna herself, if she didn't understand his intention.

Trying to shake off the pain in his head, Owyn stood. He strained to see into the darkness around him.

He could tell from the dim, wavering light that a torch or some kind of fire burned somewhere but he couldn't see it. He heard a noise like someone scuffing their feet against the cold stone. Owyn tried to move toward the bars to look through them, but the chains attached to his hands didn't extend far enough. All he could do was sit and wait.

What have I done? he thought to himself. *I've betrayed the only humans who would have defended me. I've driven away the only woman who would know me. Now, I'll be forced to live out the rest of my horrible human life in this hole. Even the army might have been better than this.*

He blinked, appalled when he realized he'd just admitted to himself he would rather live in the army as a human than in this cave-like dwelling, much like he'd lived as a dragon. Perhaps the king would see fit to exempt him from living either way.

Owyn spent time wondering where Anna was, where his human friends were, where his dragon friends were, and if anyone knew where he was. His stomach began to rumble. He stretched and flexed his muscles to keep them from tingling. No matter what position he turned to, his arms and shoulders ached.

After what felt like forever, Owyn heard movement down the hall outside his little hovel. The flickering light of fire began to grow closer.

A torch came into view and stopped outside the bars. Koris held it.

He glowered at Owyn and said nothing.

"You hit me," Owyn said. He realized how thirsty he was as his voice croaked.

"I saved your life," Koris growled.

"How do you figure?"

"Thaddius would have killed you."

Owyn nodded.

"Why did you do it?" Koris muttered, stepping closer to Owyn's confinements. "Why would you say something like that?"

Owyn shook his head, "You wouldn't understand."

"Oh no?" Koris said, his voice rising with his passion. "I've been by your side these past weeks. We've trained together. Bled together. By Tartaku, because of your accident I'm the one person you know best in this world!"

Owyn nodded, allowing his head to fall to his chest.

"So why," Koris insisted, "would you betray me and your entire claw?"

"It had nothing to do with you," Owyn answered.

"Did it have something to do with Princess Anna?"

Owyn raised his head to meet Koris's eye.

Koris nodded. "I see."

"No," Owyn said, "you don't."

"Look," Koris said, dropping his tone again. "I'm only here to try to get answers for the claw. The men wanted you dead. Princess Anna is the only reason you're still alive. If it had been anyone else, the men might have forgiven you. Even if you had insulted the king, they might have let you live."

"An insult is punishable by death?" Owyn said. If that was true, then the humans actually were as barbaric as he once thought.

"Of course not," Koris said, "but the princess. She's more beloved by the people than any other royal before her. She insists the people look her in the eye. She's kind, forgiving, and generous to everyone. She was raised in the woods and she can take care of herself, which makes her that much more admired and respected. To insult her is the greatest insult to any man who would protect her. She might forgive you, but her husband-to-be wants your head. I also can't promise any less from the men."

"What are you saying?"

"I'm saying," Koris almost whispered, "if they release you, you need to watch your back. If they don't release you, Lord Dieko will have you killed."

Owyn nodded. There was that human barbarity he recognized. The men he had lived and trained with must have been hiding it. "So, my own claw will hunt me down. Is that it?"

To Owyn's surprise, Koris paused to look off into the distance before answering. "I can't speak for our claw. Some of them want your blood, that's for sure. But mostly, it's 7-2 you have to worry about. Seems like their lieutenant pulled some strings to get them all stationed here at the castle. Some friend of Dieko's. Meanwhile, he made it sound like we were all on your side, so we're being sent to the Great Northern Mountain. 3-4 has to go where no one returns from, and 7-2 won't have to fight the dragons. Plus," Koris glanced down the hall, "if Dieko allows you to walk out of here, men loyal to him will be on top of you before you can clear the castle gate."

Owyn sagged in his chains. "No more than I deserve, I'm sure."

Koris hemmed a moment, finding something on the floor he felt the need to scrape at with his boot. "Look, Owyn," he finally said, "the claw might come around. Who knows. They know about your history. I might be able to convince them you momentarily lost your mind. But it won't work with others. Shurta knows I tried, after I knocked you out."

Owyn rubbed his head. "I'm not sure I want you doing me any other favors."

Koris shrugged. "Don't worry. Where I'm going, I won't be doing anyone favors for the rest of my short life. I'm sorry, Owyn."

Owyn nodded, slumping back against the wall again. He couldn't answer Koris as his only friend bade him farewell.

Koris walked away, taking the torch with him. The darkness swallowed Owyn. Sitting in his unforgiving cell, Owyn thought about the conversation he'd had with Ashel what seemed like a lifetime ago. She said the Star of Love would influence him. That had happened. The stars of many humans would converge on him. Yes, they never seemed to go away. Could she see his star? Did she know he needed help? And yet the more he thought about it, the more he realized that anyone searching for him would be searching for a dragon.

Owyn wallowed in the darkness for what seemed like hours. He tried to drift off to sleep, but couldn't with the worsening pain in his arms. He tried standing and stretching, but once he struggled to his feet, he knocked his head on the ceiling of the cell. His head aching even more, he finally tumbled back to sit. Listening to the moaning in the distance only worsened the thoughts that entered his mind.

As Owyn sat wondering if or how he could go back to the dragons in human form, the firelight from down the hall began moving toward him again. He could hear the sound of boots marching along the stone floor.

"Please, Highness," a man said, "he's dangerous. Slanderous and treacherous. You shouldn't—"

"Do not presume," a woman interrupted him, "to tell me what I should and shouldn't do." Owyn knew that voice.

Owyn looked up and out of the cell bars to see Anna come into view. Her sparkling green eyes were a beautiful mask of nobility. Her deep green dress took up most of the hallway, forcing the man following her to stop walking when she halted at Owyn's cell. She locked eyes with Owyn for a moment, then turned to the man.

"Open it," she snapped.

"But, Highness," the man muttered, not looking into her eyes. He was a large man, larger around the middle, but he cowered before the princess. "He's dangerous. Don't you think you should talk to him through the bars?"

"I appreciate your concern," she said without looking at him, "but I have spent all day arguing with my soon-to-be husband about this man's innocence. I won't pretend to enjoy arguing with you as well. Now, please, open the door."

The man edged around Anna's dress, producing large, clumsy keys that hung from a metal loop from his belt. When he peered out from underneath the torch, he glared down at Owyn on the floor.

Without acknowledging the man, Owyn stood as the door swung open. With the door open, Anna waited to enter. "Those," she said, speaking to the guard and pointing to Owyn's shackles, "they aren't necessary."

"But your Highness..." the man protested again.

Without waiting to hear a reason behind the guard's objection, Anna looked into Owyn's eyes. With a strict line to her mouth, she said, "You won't hurt me, will you?"

Owyn shook his head. Anna indicated for the jailer to move forward. Grumbling, he entered the cell. He picked up smaller keys on his ring to unlock the metal clasps biting into Owyn's wrist. Before stepping away, the man leaned in toward Owyn's ear. "If you so much as breathe on her in a way I don't like," he whispered, "I'll take the pleasure of giving you daily beatings."

With one final scathing glance, he stepped out of the cell into the hallway. Anna stepped into the small space. Owyn stood with his back to the wall, letting her skirts fill the room. Anna stood not quite as tall as her brother the king, but taller than most of the women Owyn had seen. She rose to her full height in the little cell, but only just. He stood with his head hunched over, the back of his head brushing the ceiling.

"Why did you say what you did?" Anna asked with curiosity, her voice not unkind. "Why would you say something like that to me?"

Owyn searched for words. How could he answer? The scowling guard watched his every move. How could he explain to Anna with him here?

"I know you," he finally said.

"I want to help you," Anna said. Did she throw her eyes over her shoulder? "I really do, but you must give me something. Lord Dieko would have you punished, more harshly than I believe necessary, but I believe everyone is allowed to feel how they will. Can you tell me? Why do you feel this way?"

She stepped closer to him, searching his eyes. He had no words. What could he say?

"Highness," the guard cautioned.

"I'm fine," Anna waved her hand at the man. She pushed closer to Owyn, pressing her skirts into his legs. "You won't hurt me, will you?" She said it loud enough for the guard to hear, but her eyes almost pleaded with Owyn's.

"No," Owyn whispered, "I would never hurt you. You know that."

Anna stepped even closer, her eyes bore into Owyn's.

"Highness," the guard pleaded impotently from the hall.

But Anna ignored him. She pressed closer. She stood nose to nose in front of Owyn. He could almost feel her breath on his face.

Her lips parted. They barely moved. If Owyn hadn't been part dragon, or formerly dragon, he might not have heard what she said. But with no more sound than a movement of the folds of her skirt, he heard her say, "Are you my Hiro?"

26

Flight

Owyn sighed. He ached to reach out to her. His heart pulled at him to embrace her and never let go. His hands shook as he forced himself not to touch her. He sucked in a breath, closed his eyes and nodded.

When he opened his eyes, he wondered if he had done something wrong. Anna's face had hardened. She pursed her lips into a line. She threw her eyes backward over her shoulder. Owyn realized she had done it on purpose. She reached her hand forward where the guard couldn't see it.

"Then," she said aloud, but she gripped Owyn's hand at the wrist, "I'm not sure if I can help you."

With a blinding fury, Anna whipped herself around, yelling at the top of her voice. She lifted Owyn's hand to her throat. As the guard fumbled forward, she used both her hands to clamp Owyn's hand around her throat, then she threw a hand forward to stop the guard's progress.

"No!" she yelled but it sounded like she couldn't breathe. Owyn tried to relax his grip on her neck, but she reached up as if to pry off his hands, only to press his fingers tighter against her throat. "Don't threaten him. It will only upset him further."

Owyn realized she was only pretending to choke since his hand was nowhere nearly tight enough around her neck to harm her. Understanding dawned as bright as day.

He tightened his grip on Anna's throat only to receive an elbow to his gut. As he doubled from the force of it, he covered the movement by grabbing her arm on the other side of his hand.

"Back up!" he yelled at the guard. "Don't make me hurt her!"

"Do as he says," Anna choked out.

As the guard backed up into the hallway, Anna and Owyn stepped out of the cell.

"Drop the keys," Owyn ordered once they were clear of the bars.

The guard hesitated.

"Do it!" Owyn yelled. He gently shook Anna, making her hair tousle.

"Ok!" As the guard took the keys from his belt and placed them on the ground in front of him, Anna threw Owyn a scathing look. The next moment, the guard looked up at them and Anna's mask of dread was back in place.

"Kick them down the hall behind you," Owyn said.

The guard pursed his lips. Owyn assumed he'd hoped to pick them up and use them against him as soon as he could.

Once the keys were as far down the hall from them as possible, Owyn pulled on Anna to back her up. "Get in," Owyn said, jerking his head toward the cell.

The man hesitated again.

"Do what he *says*!" Anna said, choking on the last word for emphasis.

"Ok, ok," the guard stepped forward, then slid into the cell.

Owyn spun Anna around so she was between the cell and Owyn. Dragging her with him, Owyn moved up the hall toward the keys, kicking the cell door shut on the guard.

"You'll never get away with this!" the man yelled from behind the bars. "You'll be hunted down by every man in the kingdom! You'll be dead in hours, traitor!"

Owyn moved down the hall until he could no longer see the guard in the cell. At the end of the hall, he pulled her into a room with a chair and a table. Three doors led out of the room, as well as a spiral staircase.

Anna fetched the keys from the floor of the hallway as soon as Owyn let go of her neck. "We have to get you out of here," she said, searching the keys. "Great Shurta, I thought you would never catch on!"

"I really am a traitor, aren't I?" Owyn watched her as she found the key she wanted and approached another door in the room.

"That doesn't matter," Anna said. "We have to get you free."

"Doesn't matter?" Owyn said. He knew he no longer had a place among either the humans or the dragons. "Where am I supposed to go?"

"Back to the dragons," Anna said. She opened the door and waved for him to go through.

"They won't have me like this," Owyn drew one hand over his very human body.

Anna punched her hands on her hips, the way Owyn had grown accustomed. "What I said about Lord Dieko was true," she said. "He'll kill you. In or out of the dungeon. With or without Philip's permission," she said. "Your only hope is to go back to the dragons."

Owyn heard another door open. Anna looked up into the rafters above them. "The other guards are coming," she whispered. "Please, hurry."

Hearing the pounding of boots, Owyn ducked into the door she held open. Anna swung in behind him, gently latching it behind her.

She leaned against the door with her eyes closed. With only sparse light seeping under the door, Owyn could barely see empty shackles, buckets, some rags, and other dungeon garbage.

"What are we doing?" he whispered. He prayed she had a better plan than hiding in a filthy closet until they were caught.

"Shh," she hissed.

Owyn heard the boots tromp down the stairs on the other side of the door. Anna retained the keys, but held the bulk of them in one hand, Owyn assumed to keep them from clanking. They could hear muffled conversation between two guards, then shouting from down the dungeon hallway.

As he listened to the sounds of movement into the hall leading to his former cell, Owyn reached for the door latch to free them. He assumed Anna planned to slip past the guards while they freed their comrades.

Anna grabbed his hand with her free hand before he could reach the latch. Holding it away from the latch, she kept her eyes and lips tightly closed. Was she counting?

They waited. After a few more counts, finally Anna's eyes sprung open. Anna reached around and clicked the door latch to open it. They both peered into the room they'd left just as the guards had reached it. It was empty.

"Hurry," she hissed before Owyn could ask any questions.

As they tip-toed through the room, Owyn looked back and saw down the hall two guards attempting to open his former cell door. Anna bolted up the circular staircase before they could notice her. Owyn followed as quickly as he could.

She didn't wait to see if anyone had followed them. She turned at the top of the stairs and ran down a corridor. "We have to get you out of here," she said again. "I'll take you out to the forest."

"And what do I do when I get there?" he asked.

Anna sighed. "You run, Owyn. That's what they call you, isn't it? Owyn?"

Owyn ran to keep up with her. "Yes," he said, "the men who found me came up with it."

Anna glanced back at him. "Seems a little simple for a dragon, doesn't it?"

He grinned. "Simple enough for a human."

She grinned back but kept running.

"How did you know?" Owyn asked as they turned another corner. "How did you know it was me?"

Anna shook her head, "No human would ever call me disgusting. Besides," she said, "I recognized your voice."

They ran down a dusty hall and up another set of stairs before they stopped at another door. Searching for the right key, Anna said, "I overheard Travaith, my brother's majishun, talking to someone about their plan." She opened the door and pushed Owyn through it. Once the door was secured behind them, she looked into his face. "You have to be careful. I tricked Travaith into believing I knew part of the plan. He let slip that a dragon informed the faeries of the danger of flarote to their species. He said it was used in the poison because it is fatal if a dragon eats too much. Is that true?"

Owyn's teeth ground together. Anna didn't say anything. She pursed her lips and nodded, then led him down the hall again.

After following a labyrinth of hallways, they finally came to another locked door. Owyn felt exposed as he looked up and down the long corridor on either side of them.

"It was a dragon," he mumbled as Anna fumbled with the keys until she found the right one. He paused. "A dragon betrayed dragons. Who would do such a thing?"

"Quickly," Anna grabbed Owyn by the shirt and pulled him through the doorway.

Before falling after her, he saw firelight at the end of the hallway. The sound of men shouting echoed down the hall.

Owyn closed the door behind him, but Anna was already working the keys on another door at the base of a tower.

"The guards on the tower will see you as you run into the forest," she said as the lock clicked in place. "But as long as you get to the forest, you should be fine. Their arrows won't reach you. Wait until you're in the trees to change."

"Change?" The word caught him so off-guard he stumbled. "What do you mean 'change'?"

"Change back into a dragon," Anna said. She looked at him as if it was understood.

Owyn scrunched his eyebrows. "I don't know that I can," he said. "I don't know how or why this happened in the first place."

Anna threw the latch home, opening the last doorway out to the fading sunlight in the trees beyond. "Then you'll have to figure it out. You won't get away from here as a human. If you can get to the trees, you can fly out of here. You'll be far enough away that—"

"Explain on the way," he said as he bolted through the door. He grabbed her hand to pull her into the forest with him, but got jerked back.

Anna shook her head, gazing into his eyes. "I can't. I have to get married. It's the only way Philip will trust me. It's the only way he'll tell me anything."

"No, you don't," he searched for words. What was it worth being a human if he couldn't be with the human he loved? "Don't you see?" he said, "we can be together. You don't have to do anything."

"Don't," she said, squeezing his hand. "You have to go."

The sound of men's voices behind them grew louder, but he stared into her green eyes, gripping her fingers as a life line.

"Please," she said, pulling one of her hands free. Tears leaked from her eyes.

"You choose him," Owyn said. His heart ached. His stomach burned.

Anna reached into a fold on the side of her skirts. Men pounded on the door behind her. She threw herself against the door, keeping her hand in the pocket. Blocking the door with her body, she looked up into his face and said, "Hiro, go."

Grass and twigs crunched under his boots. He looked down to see his legs pumping under him. Men shouted behind him in pursuit. They would never catch up. The forest trees crowded over his head. His legs burned at the speed. They burned almost as much as his belly burned. She'd made him go. She'd made him leave her. She'd chosen to stay and marry the human.

And why shouldn't she? he thought. *I'm a dragon.*

Flame exploded inside him. His legs flew through the forest as his wings ripped from his back and his claws extended. He didn't wait for an opening in the trees, Hiro threw himself past the branches into the sky.

27

Revelations

Hiro crashed into the ground, rolling to a stop. He almost felt like a fledgling learning how to fly again.

He hadn't stopped flying until this moment and he felt like he had forgotten how to land as well. He lay on the ground, panting. A dragon had betrayed all the dragons. Anna had chosen not to be with him.

No, he shook himself, *that thought almost killed me.*

He felt the fire in his belly gutter again. Whenever he thought of Anna, the fire threatened to go out. It had once, while he flew over the Torthoth mountains. When his thoughts drifted to Anna, his body had changed back into a human. In mid-air. Terrified of falling to his death and aching to be with the dragons, the fire in his belly ignited. He had barely turned back into a dragon again before hitting the trees.

I have to get this under control, he thought as he lay under the trees next to Centaur River. The smell of clean dirt soaked his nostrils. He could smell plants, trees, small woodland animals, even centaurs and dragons. The human stench had all but drained from his mind. It felt so good to be back in the wild again. His fatigue began to overtake him. He was safe. He was free. He could return home.

As his eyes began to close, Hiro heard hooves clopping against the dirt. But something else was with them. Claws. Dragons. All of them ran together. Toward Hiro.

"Hiro!" Tog burst through the trees, not even attempting to hide his excitement. "You're alive!" He swung his tail around, slapped Hiro on the neck knocking his head to the side, then pounced on him.

"I knew it!" Prak yelled as he, Maggoran, Ashel, Vikal, and several other centaurs barreled through the trees behind Tog. "Ashel said you couldn't be dead! She said your star was surrounded by humans. In fact, she said your star had changed! She said it looked dangerous. But I didn't believe it. You look the same as you always did. A little more tired, but a good night's rest will take care of that. Where have you been?"

"Yes," Ashel said, throwing her arms around Hiro's neck before Tog could pounce on him again. "You gave us all a good scare. Where have you been?"

They all stared at him expectantly. He'd been gone for weeks. How was he going to explain that?

"I was injured," he hemmed.

When he didn't continue, Maggoran said, "Yes, Hiro. I showed them my memory. But how did you escape?"

All eyes were on him. Why hadn't he thought of a good story for this moment before coming home?

"I...found a place to hide," he said.

Maggoran squinted at him. "You've been hiding for almost an entire moon cycle?"

Hiro shrugged. "I had to wait for the humans to leave and I wanted to make sure they were gone."

Prak cocked his head to the side. "Did *they* stay in one place for the entire moon cycle? Because we've been hunting down the humans and the faeries and they have definitely never stayed in one place for long! In fact, they seem to keep on the move. Unless, of course they're camped near the Rock Clouds. The Courageous Kingdom is there now. In the country north of the Rock Clouds—"

Prak took a breath before continuing, but Ashel stepped forward, giving him a glance. "We have many enemies approaching, Hiro. It's a dangerous time to be a dragon."

Hiro nodded. "I need to speak to you," he nodded to Tog, "and you. Alone."

"And we need to speak with you as well," Ashel said. "But I think Prak should join us. After all, he's been leading the dragons and the centaurs in your absence."

Hiro's eyes popped open. He looked to see the little brown dragon puff out his chest and nod at Ashel with a grin.

Hiro turned to Tog, whom he had assumed would take over matters while he was gone. But Tog nodded, "Prak's done a fine job keeping everyone organized."

Hiro smiled. "Well done, Prak," he said. "You can stay as well."

Ashel trotted over to Maggoran and Vikal, instructing them to take the others back to their camp.

"One of the lookouts saw you," she told Hiro as the others loped back into the trees. "We came as quickly as we could to find you. But we've had no luck all these weeks. We haven't found any of the poisoned arrows."

"We've attacked every supply station and caravan we've found," Prak said. "We can't seem to find anything. We don't know what's wrong."

"I do," Hiro said. All three of their heads lifted. "There's a traitor."

He leaned over in front of Tog, placing his nose in front of his best friend. He remembered Anna in the dungeon, telling him a dragon gave up the one piece of information that a dragon should never reveal. His fire guttered ever so slightly, but it subsided quickly for him to breathe hot air into Tog's face.

Tog sat back without blinking. "What's wrong?" he said.

"Didn't you get the memory?" Hiro asked.

"Nothing."

I can't pass on human memories, Hiro realized. His fire guttered again, but again, Hiro had no need to breathe fire to reignite it.

"Are you ok, Hiro?" Ashel asked.

"What did those monsters do to you?" Prak growled.

"I'm fine," Hiro lied. "We have more important things to discuss. Someone told me a dragon passed on the information that flarote can kill a dragon."

Prak's mouth dropped open. Ashel gasped. Tog's toggling eyes dilated.

"Who would do this?" Tog whispered.

"How do you know it was a dragon?" Ashel asked.

"It's a long story," Hiro said. "One I had hoped to pass along without speaking."

"Well," Ashel put her hands on her withers, "you would have to tell me anyway."

Hiro looked between her and Tog. "I'm not sure I can."

Tog dipped his head, then lifted it to Hiro's. "Did this come from...?" He didn't finish the question, but Hiro knew what he was asking. Hiro nodded.

"Well," Ashel's huge eyes bounced between the three dragons, "it sounds like you have a lot to tell Prak and me."

Hiro and Tog shared a glance. Tog nodded. "Alright," Hiro faced the accusing eyes of Prak and Ashel, "the whole story is..." he glanced at Tog for encouragement. Tog nodded again. "I only survived because I'm friends with a human woman."

Prak's maw dropped open again. But Ashel stepped closer. "What human woman?" she asked.

Tog rolled an eye watching Hiro and waved a claw at Ashel. Hiro gathered what courage he could, and said, "Princess Anna."

Silence.

"And we're supposed to what? Trust her?" Ashel shouted.

"That's what I said," Tog muttered.

Hiro threw a scathing look at Tog, but turned back to the others. "I trust her with my life and she's saved it. Several times," he admitted.

Ashel threw her hands into the air and tromped around in a circle. Before she could make a full circle, Hiro turned to Prak. "Prak," he said, "have you nothing to say?"

Prak searched the ground, the trees, Ashel's eyes, the ground, Tog, and finally rested on Hiro. "You realize what you're asking," he said. "You're telling us we can't trust dragons and faeries, but we can trust humans. Do you have any idea how that sounds?"

"I know how it sounds," Hiro said, "but I'm not asking you to trust every human. I certainly don't." He thought of the men in Squad 3-4. He had trusted them, with his life if necessary. But only with his human life. The fire in his belly shook, but didn't threaten to quench, so he continued. "And it's only one dragon that is deceiving us. We need to figure out who it is and why."

"No," Prak shook his head. "No, Hiro, *you* need to figure out who it is and why. The rest of us will spend our time defending our home and those we care about." He looked at each of them in turn. Hiro realized how much Prak had changed since he'd left. His young voice had a stern edge to it. "This information doesn't leave this group." Ashel opened her mouth to speak, but Prak cut her off. "No, Ashel, you can't tell Joss or Rylan. Or Vikal. Maybe that will change with time, but for now they don't need to know. We will continue doing what we can to stop the humans from attacking. Rakgar will continue his brand of diplomacy with the faeries. And Hiro, you will discover what you can about the traitor's identity. Bring any information to one of us."

"What about—" Tog started.

"No!" Prak barked. "We can't tell Rakgar or Surneen or anyone we're supposed to be able to trust. The only beings we can trust are the ones in this group. Hiro will be on his own to figure out who the traitor is, and we'll continue as if we know nothing about it."

Ashel nodded. "That is the best way to flush a traitor," she said.

"Alright," Hiro nodded, "how are you going to stop the humans?"

Ashel and Prak nodded to each other. "Right," Prak said, "come with us."

The three turned back toward the forest where Vikal and the others had disappeared. As they turned, Ashel began to explain where she knew the groups of humans were from as far as they had already scouted. While she spoke, Hiro's mind drifted to Anna. Instead of following his friends, he swung his long neck to look out over the trees on the other side of the river. He couldn't see the mountains that hid the only woman he would ever love, but he felt the tug at his heart increasingly pulling him toward her.

Without warning, the fire in his belly ceased. Cool air brushed Owyn's naked skin. He jerked his head back to the others before they could turn to see him.

No, he thought in a panic, *keep your mind and body here. In this moment. If they see me, they'll kill me without even first considering what's happening.*

As Tog's head swung around, Hiro's belly burned hot as coal.

Tog lilted his head. "Are you coming, Hiro?"

Hiro took a deep breath. "Yes," he mustered, "just tired."

"Plan first," Ashel said.

"Rest when you're dead," Prak finished.

Hiro nodded and loped after them.

If I don't get this changing body under control, he thought, *I'll rest sooner than I would like.*

The adventure will conclude in

the Krusible of Avonoa

Book Five in the Avonoa Series!!

Acknowledgments

I'd like to say thank you to everyone who has helped me put together this fourth book.

Thank you, Sue Goolsby, the best darn editor a girl could ask for! Thank you for teaching me so much from your work. Thank you for your patience and dedication. Thank you for keeping me and my commas in order!

Thank you to Kay Cooper McMahon for your amazing art work! Thank you for sticking with me and sharing your talent. You are a wonderful artist and even better friend!

Thank you also to my beta readers. Ben, Jason, Jessica, Jillian, Josh, Loury, Tifani. I couldn't have done it without all of you!

Thank you to my dad for proofreading for me. Thank you for helping me polish!

Thank you to my family and friends and everyone who has kept up with Avonoa! Your support is beyond anything I could have hoped for! There are great things to come in the final installation of the adventure in Avonoa!

69383880R00174

Made in the USA
Columbia, SC
15 August 2019